SPOOK LIGHTS

Southern Gothic Horror

Eden Royce

For the ladies of 119, for… well, everything.

SPOOK
LIGHTS

Praise for Spook Lights

Eden Royce delivers a sultry and spicy dose of Southern Gothic. The stories are rich in flavor and clever in metaphor, the horrors completely surreal or—far more unnerving—all too possible. She brings a refreshing perspective to the table that paranormal lovers are sure to enjoy.

—B.D. Bruns, author of The Gothic Shift

This book is a collection of Southern Gothic short stories, a specific and rare type of horror fiction. What is the difference, you may ask? If a horror story is a man in a mask, chasing a woman through a dark forest with a bloody axe, these stories are the warm embrace of a long lost lover as he slowly drags her down into his grave. A true gothic is dripping with atmosphere, history, and depth. It sneaks up on you when you feel warm and safe, then touches your emotions and psyche in a place that will leave you scarred for life.

A gothic story of any type is not easy to pull off. It takes a gentle hand, a fist in a velvet glove, if you will. With a skillful hand she guides the reader through all of these experiences.

This is a beautiful and unique collection which should be a treasured addition to any library.

—Roma Gray, author of Gray Shadows Under a Harvest Moon

Table of Contents

Introduction

I labored over the title for this collection of stories. When I first decided to release them in one book, I wasn't sure how to unite them under one theme. Of course, they are dark tales, but possibly not in the vein currently popular. What you will find is subtle—often times called quiet—horror.

My favorite kind.

Oh, don't get me wrong. I love a good jump or quiver now and then. But Gothic horror has always been my favorite. Maybe because moody Gothic horror is the first kind I remember experiencing. Sitting at home with my mother and grandmother watching an old black and white horror classic on TV was how I spent many a night growing up.

We Southerners are born storytellers, so naturally I wanted to create my own stories as I got older. But I had a desire to see characters that reflected my background, and I didn't find too many. After I began writing my own work, I found the next step was to get it out in the public eye. Before submitting any of my tales to publishers, one of the first decisions I had to make was to place my work in a genre, a category that defined it. I struggled there as well. Many of my stories weren't considered true horror to publishers—there were no lavishly described squicky killings, no serial killers. My style of writing almost seemed to suit another era, one that was long gone.

However, I soon found Southern Gothic, a genre of writing that is about the Southern mystique (and I don't think that's too grandiose a term). Southern Gothic is a subset of its parent Gothic style of writing, a style that places characters in situations focused on the strange, the grotesque, the macabre. It's these atmospheric settings that give Gothic writing its definitive sound and feel.

Typically, Southern Gothic gets the added distinction of having a setting that in itself can conjure up images of horror for some: slavery, lynchings, war. If asked to sum up this genre of writing, I would turn to James Baldwin, one of my favorite poets, and use his quote: "The South is very beautiful but its beauty makes one sad because the lives that people live here, and have lived here, are so ugly."

There is a history in the title of this collection. The ugly part of that history is why I was at war with myself over using the title *Spook Lights*. For years, the word "spook" has been used as a racial slur for a black person. Groundbreaking author Sam Greenlee embraced the term and used it in his 1969 spy novel, *The Spook Who Sat by the Door*, now required reading at the FBI academy. Greenlee's novel is the story of Dan Freeman, the first black CIA officer—spook also being a slang term for spy. I recognize the history of the word, but it holds an additional meaning for me.

I grew up in Charleston, South Carolina, a world-renowned tourist city, known for her hospitality and rightly so. Even her nickname, the Holy City, inspires thoughts of serene charm. She has that in abundance, as many writers, Southern and not, have noted over the years. I've read a great deal of these authors and enjoy their work. Much of it focuses on the gentry—old South royalty—and I admit to being fascinated by their stories myself. Turning back the guise of propriety and revealing well-hidden secrets and shame is alluring, but in those tales, not many people of color are featured as protagonists. They are incidental characters that flit in and out of tales, rarely memorable in their own right.

Charleston's dark side is illustrious. There is a popular tour of the city that focuses on prostitution, bootleg whiskey, crimes in the names of love and money. But there too, people of color make few appearances. My aim was to create and bring together stories— dark fiction smattered with a touch of magical realism—and depict the Holy City from the perspective I grew up with: fiery women, conjure magic, and a healthy appreciation of and respect for the unknown.

A peninsula, Charleston is surrounded on three sides by water and most of the undeveloped areas are covered in marshland. On certain hot, humid nights, when you look out over the marsh, you can see ethereal lights. They flicker as though they are lanterns, and coyly recede when you try to approach them. Some cultures call them wills-o'-the-wisp or fairy fire and they are feared as a portent of death. However, my grandmother called them spook lights. I asked her once what they were and she said that some people say they're ghost lights, emanating from lost spirits wandering the earth. Then she whispered close to my ear that others believed them to be guides and they were the lights slaves followed years ago deep into the dank marshes and away to freedom.

I always chose to believe my grandmother's explanation and it has stuck with me all these years. Although I have now moved to England, I thought it appropriate to release a collection of dark tales inspired by the city where I grew up, the place that shaped me. And my dark thoughts.

Dum Spiro Spero, Charleston. I miss y'all.

~Eden Royce

Kent, England

2015

The Watered Soul

The juke joint was jumping when Lucius Blacksmoke slipped in. Outside it didn't look like much, just a run-down former fish shack perched on the edge of the Charleston marsh surrounded by biting flies and stealthy gators. Even with the sun descending from its perch, the heat was stifling; its dying rays still scorched the skin left bare by his seersucker suit.

He'd spent over six years looking for the woman who'd cursed him. Each time he'd come close—in Paris, in Berlin—Lucius had somehow missed her. Usually, it was by days, but once in Tunisia, he'd missed her by hours. But now, after following countless tales of healing magics across the globe, he'd traced her here at considerable cost to his pocket and himself.

Sometimes, it was good to surround yourself with drunks. They told stories no one believed in the clear light of day. One such man told him of a woman running a watering hole. "Best thing you evah drank. Felt like I was lifted up." Lucius listened, slowing his drinking enough to remain more sober than his companion and only then long enough to record the details of her location. Now here he was.

Inside the ramshackle establishment was no better. Dust motes floated on the few shafts of light that pierced the heavy dimness. The smell of sweat and musk from gyrating bodies and the floor shaking from the efforts of the quartet and their brand of dirty jazz were enough to make him wish for the quiet serenity of home, although no one there would know him now. He much preferred the music of his own people, music of elegance and meter, first played to him as a young man by their composers—Bach and Handel and their counterparts—on his father's harpsichord. The sound of this discordant clanging burrowed into his skull, making

1

his vision narrow and grow black at the edges. Every part of him itched to flee, but his desire pushed him forward.

Lucius choked down the thick, odorous air, trying to settle his protesting stomach as he searched the room. A biscuit-colored woman stood in the middle of the room on a make shift stage, no more than a few two-by-fours with a plywood top nailed in place, belting out raunchy lyrics in a sandpaper alto. His gaze flicked over her form-fitting dress, damp with sweat under the arms and breasts, and then away. Behind her, a dusty-looking black man in battered overalls dragged a bow across a fiddle that had never seen a good day. And the drummer—

—was a woman.

Lucius stared. Even now, the woman he sought wouldn't follow the traditions of the Hutu tribe she'd grown up with. The waterfall of tears Hutu had shed when she'd left her village hand in hand with him made Lucius—then called William—waver in his intentions on that day so long ago. But now he questioned her devotion since she was allowing this female to batter away at an instrument her people only intended for a man's hand. Bet she's proud of herself, he thought, eyes narrowing in anger as well as pain. He shook off the notion. For some reason when he thought of Hutu, he saw her naiveté, fresh and unspoiled. But too much had happened for her to maintain that tenderness.

He strolled over to a decrepit metal washtub serving as an ice bucket across from the stage and slipped the hunting knife from his pocket. He hid his opening of the blade under a fumble around in the basin for a few cool chips of ice to suck on. Any sound was lost under the twanging banjo and the foot stomping of the crowd, their bodies sour and rank from exertion. Day laborers that hadn't moved far from the plantations. They'd been given freedom and they still clung to massa's teat. His smirk stayed in place as his gaze found Hutu.

2

She was seated across the room with a drink before her, her cherry wood skin blending into the shadows. The woman grasped a fragment of ice from the glass with her red fingernails, and dropped it down the front of her poppy printed dress. With a shudder, she met his gaze. Hutu watched Lucius while he strolled across the rickety dance floor, the knife concealed in his sleeve, and stopped in front of the overturned whisky barrel she used as a table.

"When you left the last time, it took me three years and Jesus to get over you."

He laughed. "You got Jesus and you drinkin' in a juke joint?" The accent he'd practiced over the years to get past the "locals only" mentalities in some of these backwater towns sounded weak and limp next to hers, an affectation gone wrong. Even his suit felt awkward somehow, too prosperous, too light, in this place of darkness. As he'd expected, Hutu looked as though she belonged. Her eyes, heavy lidded, watched him. Her perspiration kissed skin was bare of makeup, but smooth and unlined, even though he knew she was older than he.

"I own this place, Lucius, so yes, I'm here. Most of the time." She picked up the now empty glass and shook it above her head. "Artie, one more," she yelled over the jiving dancers. An old man, face shiny dark like a new tire, raised a hand in acknowledgement. When she looked at Lucius again it was with undisguised hatred. "Where were you? Out there on the street somewhere being with who you please after I gave you—"

"Gave me what?" His voice quaked and his tongue tripped over the thickening words in his mouth. "What'd you give me?"

"A gift. Nothing you didn't ask for—nothing you didn't want. But it was something I should have never done." She took a slender cigarette from a gold case and blew on the end. It flared into life and she placed the filtered tip between her plump lips and drew deeply.

3

His head thumped now, the music drilling down into his brain. The drum brought back images of wide leafed flora and weighty, moist heat. It was easy to see why Hutu chose this place to call home. The tiny makeshift huts along the river here were so like the ones he'd found her in, barefoot and bare breasted. Where she'd danced with abandon to the cacophony ebbing from the taut goatskin drums, her nipples hard and dark as blackcurrants.

The rhythm coming from this drum eclipsed all the other instruments. Lucius felt like he had blinders on: all he saw was Hutu in front of him and the rest of the world faded into darkness. He pressed his head down into one hand, the knife in his sleeve pricking lightly at his wrist, ready. Ready to reclaim his life from before. He dropped into the chair opposite her with a grunt, sitting down hard.

"You know," she said casually, as if she were talking to someone at the market, commenting on what was fresh from the fields. "One time way back, the soul was thought to be a mix of fire and water. The goal of life was supposed to be getting that water outta your soul. Become pure fire." She blew smoke daggers at him.

"How?" he managed, panting under the assault of percussion. Through all of his lifetimes, he hadn't felt pain like this. The drum, its tone high-pitched and resonant, seemed to seek out and attack his weakest parts, piercing him.

"That's a question you should have asked me before you drank the elixir of life." She held the empty glass up to her eye and peered at him through it, catching the dregs of fading light.

Lucius swept his arm over the table, sending an ashtray and her cigarette case clattering to the floor, each hand-rolled tube scattering in a different direction. "You should have told me what it would do!" There was no pause in the dancing. *Jump. Spin. Stomp.*

Artie refilled Hutu's glass.

4

"If I had known you wanted the secret of eternity, I could have bargained with you for a fair price. There was no need for you to make a fool of me. You knew what you were in for. Only thing you didn't know was each time you came back... each time—" She broke off and leaned back in the chair, her face thoughtful. "Now I know why I was supposed to stay a virgin. Untouched. My father said that was the only way the magic would work. He was wrong, though. It still works, only differently."

"Just...fix this." He beat against his temple with a fist. That sound, like insects boring into his brain seeking nourishment. "Please."

Hutu looked at him, her brown-black eyes not missing a hair on his head as half of the whisky disappeared down her long throat. "Hm. Like I was saying. A dry soul is best. It's worldly pleasures that make the soul moist." She chuckled softly, but the sound carried to his ears, winding easily through the efforts of the band. "Yours must be drowning."

"You don't understand me, Anna Lee," he said, calling her by the name he had given her a hundred—no, over two hundred now—years before. He'd never been able to pronounce her given name, the one bestowed on her by the tribe that banned her from their midst because of him. *Umulaazi,* they had yelled in their clipped, guttural language. *She has lain with the pale stranger.* Her father had been the last to turn his back to her.

Lucius had paid for another ticket to bring her to the Continent with him. He had held her as she wept for what she had lost, rocking her in time to the sway of the ship. When they reached land months later, he'd left her. "I'm the kind of man... Dammit, I need things, woman!"

"So I see." Her eyes flicked over his limp suit.

5

"Don't you mock me, she-witch." Lucius rubbed his sleeve over his mouth, smearing sweat and mucus. "What was I supposed to do?"

She shrugged. "Oh, I don't know. Be happy?"

Lucius grabbed her glass and downed the remaining amber liquid. The whiskey seared his throat and he wanted to claw it back out. *Would he ever get enough of drinking? Would he ever get tired of existing?* The liquid boiled in his belly, mixing the stench of his sickly sweat with the perspiration from the dancers on the floor and on the tables. All of it set to the rhythm of the forbidden drum.

"No, not you. You couldn't be happy," Her voice surrounded him and he felt hot shame build and creep up his chest to his neck. "Contentment is not in your nature." She motioned for another drink. "Something you never knew was how you hurt me. Each time you came back dirty, torn up, stinking of bathtub liquor, I took you in. But it hurt me."

"I never meant—"

Hutu's voice lost its cool, disinterested tone. It thundered out of her like a Baptist preacher's brimstone sermon, vibrating the walls. She trembled. "Each time I touched you, I could see them, the women you ran with. When I picked up your shirt to wash it, I could see each one… see their faces as you took them. Touched them."

The music slowed, deepened into a pulsing, and the dancers responded without changing steps. *Jump. Stomp. Sliiide…*

Hutu dropped the spent cigarette into the empty glass. "A root lady told me one time she could help me. Surprised she didn't want to live forever too. But she wanted something else."

He nodded. "That's good." His throat felt thick, coated with flannel. "You don't need some witch woman giving you anything. They always want something and it's never good."

6

"But I did give it to the old thing. What she wanted. Because I have a soft spot for people in need." Her eyes pinned him. "Did you know the elixir can create life as well as extend it?"

A fly buzzed in his ear and he waved it away. Undaunted, the insect returned, its threadlike legs tickling the side of his neck. Hutu leaned forward on the makeshift table, gold bracelets jingling like wind chimes.

He gripped the knife. This was it, what he had come for. *Be strong, now.*

All he saw was her staring at him, ready to claim her vengeance. It had taken over two hundred years for him to come crawling to her, asking—begging—for help. Or was it mercy? Two hundred years since he'd brought her to this country as his property and then sold her. Her screaming and wailing and the thump of drumbeats. In his head, still there after all this time. In truth, the sounds were always there, following him from life to life and person to person. He'd been William, and David, and Franklin trying to wedge his way into the lives of the upper class and failing each time. This time around, he'd chosen to be Lucius, a smaller fish in a smaller pond, in his attempt to prosper. No matter who he was, the noises stayed in his mind, hovering like a nosy aunt. What relief he found lay in drowning himself in strong drink and soft women.

Eternity. He'd wanted those years to get rich, take advantage of the eons of time spread out before him to prosper. Get smart and strong and important. But it hadn't happened. He'd asked for his body to live forever, but he hadn't asked for strength of character. He drank and threw money after horses and dice and whores. He'd adopted persona after persona in an attempt to enjoy his gift. There was always another tomorrow to become great. Plenty of time, he'd thought.

She'd never told him what it would be like. That he'd have to live with himself and his choices throughout all time. That no identity change would ever allow him to escape who and what he really was.

He pulled what was left of his fading vision to focus on Hutu and saw her smiling broadly, her teeth blindingly white, as if she knew his thoughts. And she may have. His anger flared again as she lit another cigarette. Lucius lifted his arm and struck down with the knife, polished and sharp, intent on ending his torment. To end the magic, you must kill its creator.

A yell pierced the air, loud and masculine. Almost blind from the music, he hadn't seen old man Artie return to sit another drink in front of Hutu, to replacing the one Lucius had guzzled in defiance. Lucius looked down, vision reduced to almost nothing, and saw three thick brown fingers on the overturned barrel table, leaking red. Artie pulled his hand to his chest and hurried away, leaving his severed brown fingers behind. In that moment Lucius realized his error. It took him a few more moments of sweeping his gaze from one corner of the joint to the other to realize he could see clearly.

The music had stopped.

All attention—from the dancers, from the band, from the drinkers—was directed at him. Their laughter bubbled up like salted water in a pot, filling the juke.

"I know what you want, Lucius. You got your eternity and now you're tired of it." Her laugh joined the other chuckles. "Your stupid little game of suicide was beneath you. It was certainly beneath me." Artie's crimson blood twisted down into the glass of rye whiskey, then dissipated in the amber liquid. Hutu pulled a clean white handkerchief from her bosom and carefully placed each finger inside before wrapping the bundle tightly. Someone, likely one of the dancers, spirited the grisly package away to the corner where Artie now crouched. "What was I supposed to do when you slashed at me, get angry and kill you? Oh, please."

8

He felt the resolve flee from him like roaches from bright light. "I'm tired, Anna Lee. Tired of…everything."

Hutu nodded. "I know, Sugar. But you couldn't do it, could you? Not on your own." She leaned over the rickety barrel turned table and took his face in one hand. Her skin smelled like sandalwood and newly formed ash. "Do you want me to help you?"

"I'm sorry." His voice was soft, near inaudible, and his shoulders slumped.

"I know that too." She stubbed the cigarette out in her hand, leaving a tiny circle of ashes in her palm before she took hold of his fingers in her smaller ones.

Fire seeped from her fingers and engulfed their joined hands, bringing a rich glow to the now stoic faces surrounding the pair. The flames grew around both of them, sparking and arcing, purifying his flesh and muscle and bone. Liquid pain flowed through him. He flinched but did not pull away from the searing heat. Lucius sagged under the weight of their combined gazes, but once again, he only had eyes for the woman holding his fate in flame-drenched hands.

"Impuzamugambi," he said, her name falling from his lips for the first time.

Her smile was tender as the room filled with steam.

Doc Buzzard's Coffin

It took three of us to get Doc Buzzard in the coffin.

Mama had his arms, I had his feet, and Jay had his narrow shoulder under Doc's backside, propping it up. Wasn't just that he was heavy, but it was black as an ant's hiney in our backyard and hard to see. Trees covered most of the land out here allowing tiny slices of moonlight to slide through. The night was quiet, like all the crickets and frogs had stopped singing to watch what the Turner family was doing.

Plus it was hot as fire out here in the marsh and the mosquitoes were biting me twice as fast because I didn't have a free hand to swat at them. Even though it was nighttime, heat still lay over everything like an itchy blanket. Marsh gases bubbled in front of us, smelling like a match blown out.

Gran's old kerosene lantern was the only other light. The lantern swung on an iron pole shoved into the moist black dirt—good growing soil—and the watery beam cut a narrow path that disappeared into the darkness each time Doc's body swung toward it. The soft light wiggled like candle fire and I could barely make out the white paint on our little clapboard house at the end of the dirt road if I stretched on my tiptoes and learned over.

The body swung again and the glow from the lantern hit Doc's face and I swore I saw him smile. Sweat ran down my face and arms, making my hands so wet and slippery I almost dropped my share of Doc's weight. He was dressed in dusty dungarees and a worn out work shirt with the name patch torn off it. He was barefoot and the bottoms of his feet were the same burned toast color as the rest of him and felt thick but smooth as a worn-out tire. Paying so much attention to Doc I tripped over my own feet, but I didn't fall.

"Ow, Jezzie. Watch out."

I hissed at my twin brother. "Quiet. You think we're out here picking cotton?"

"That ain't even funny." His voice was higher than mine even though we were both almost thirteen. "It's your fault we're doing this."

"No, it ain't." We kept plenty of secrets from other people, but never from each other. Telling his secret was the hardest thing I ever had to do. My belly squeezed when I thought about it. I took a deep breath of that matchstick air and tried not to think too much.

His voice hardened around his whisper. "You should a kept your mouth shut."

"I tried to." I could feel my face get even hotter than it already was in the sticky heat.

"Both of you keep your mouths shut. This ain't nothing to play with." Mama's pretty dark curls had already melted from the moist air. She hefted Doc's shoulders higher on her chest. His body dropped to one side and Mama scrambled to catch his arm and shift him back into place. We kept shuffling with ol' Doc, getting him to the coffin where it lay open on the ground next to a mound of dirt.

I got his feet in and then helped Jay push in most of Doc's weight. We were trying to fix the body real good and neat in the box when headlights came over the rise toward our farm.

"Shit," I said.

"Jezebel!" Mama still managed to scold me at a time like this. "It's just Larry John. Always late. Should a already been here helping us with this mess." She dropped Doc's head into the coffin with a *thunk*.

Larry John was sweet on Mama. That was the only reason he said he would help us tonight. But I knew it couldn't be him.

12

"Help! He got me, Mama!" Jay screamed like the Devil had him turned cross his knee. He pulled and yanked against the pine box but he kept getting jerked back.

"Lord, James. Doc ain't got hold of nobody right now." Mama grabbed his arm and held him still while she followed the frayed denim strap of Jay's overalls and wedged it out from under the witchdoctor. "Now, hush that foolishness," she said.

I got that bad feeling again. The one where my head felt light and my heart started beating real fast. Mama said it was my nerves, but I could tell it made her scared when I felt it. So I didn't tell her anymore.

"Uh, Mama? That don't look like Larry John's truck."

Mama looked up as the lamplight hit the slow-moving police car.

"Shit," she said.

"Run," I said to Jay.

"Don't move," Mama said, straightening up her back and dusting off her hands on her house dress. "Neither one of you move a hair. Turners don't run from nobody."

The police car pulled up right alongside of us. The headlights were so bright it made my eyes water. We all waited like statues while the door creaked open and Deputy Darryl "Dog" Collins waddled out. I wrinkled my nose at the smell of stale cigarettes that came out when he opened the car door.

I called him Dog because he had a mashed in face and big floppy cheeks like a bloodhound. And he was always showing up where he thought he smelled something.

"Damn." Me and Mama said it at the same time.

Jay backed up against me, his close-cropped head just in front of where my chest was. I was glad he did because it hid the fact I was getting to be a lady.

"Well, now. Evening, Miss Janey. Children." His skin was pasty and shiny with sweat.

Mama's back was stiffer than old Doc's. "Deputy Collins." She threw a look at us and we both mumbled a greeting. Getting caught burying a body was no reason to forget your manners.

"Sure is a nice night. Little late in the season for planting, though."

"Why you here, Collins?"

"Is that any way for someone such as yourself to address an officer of the law?"

Mama put on her best talking-to-white-people voice. "To what do I owe the *pleasure* of your visit?"

"I think you know." He walked up to the crude pine box and shined his flashlight inside. "Got a phone call something was going on at the Turner place, so I made sure to get myself straight down here."

"Who called?"

"I'm afraid I can't divulge that information."

Mama put her hands on her hips. Deputy Dog's eyes followed the movement. "Where's Larry John?"

"Oh, I suspect he's having himself a little late night snack somewhere. Maybe with a lady friend." He turned to us kids. "You know, Officer LeRoy's wife made a fine bunch of ginger cookies today. I bet he'd give your Ma a few."

"She ain't done nothing wrong," I said.

"Oh no? She's standing in the yard 'round close to midnight with her brother's dead body in a handmade coffin." He hitched up his pants at the waist. "I'd say that was plenty. Plenty of somethin'."

"He ain't dead!" Jay shouted.

I put my hand in my pocket. When I rubbed my doll's rough cloth body, its crepe wool hair wrapped around my fingers and I felt better.

"Hush up, both of you," Mama said.

The deputy looked at each of us in turn. "Now don't tell me no hoodoo voodoo stories about how Doc is gonna wake up soon because he's just tired from some spell wearing him out." He reached into the box, pushing his fat fingers along Doc's neck. "I might not be no doctor, but I do know if a man's heart don't beat, he's dead."

Jay squirmed and shifted from foot to foot. I put my hands on his shoulders 'cause it felt like he was thinking about running off, in spite of what Mama said. With a couple of squeezes, the tightness was gone and he leaned back against me.

"There a question in there somewhere, Deputy?"

"I'm smelling something and the time ain't come when my nose is wrong. You got this last chance to come clean with me, Janey. What happened here tonight?"

"Oh, so it's Janey, now?"

"This is serious and I need to know what's going on. Did Larry John put his hands on you? Then Doc tried to step in and he killed him? That ain't really your fault. A woman can make a man do some wild things."

15

"You crazy?" Mama pushed one of her limp black curls off her forehead, when it fell back down again, she tucked it behind her ear.

"Though I understand how you could drive a man to do things that wasn't the usual." The lamplight danced around with the car headlights as the deputy grinned and adjusted his uniform pants.

"I told you nothin's wrong."

The deputy went over to his police car and opened the back door. "Well, then you won't mind telling that to the Sheriff."

Mama said nothing. Just walked over to that car like she was the Queen of Sheba and got right on in. We followed.

"Where you two going?" Deputy Dog asked me.

"With Mama," I said. "We ain't got nobody else."

***

I was kinda disappointed nobody was locked up when we got to the police station. The jail cells were all empty but the bars looked like they had fresh paint. Big wood desks like the ones school principals had lined up along two walls. One of those new air conditioner things was in one window, but it sounded like it was struggling to breathe. The whole place smelled like man sweat and burnt coffee.

Sheriff Edwards was the tallest man I'd ever seen. He pulled his hat off and ducked to come in the meeting room in the back of the police station with me and Mama and Jay. His brown hair was damp around the edges where the hat had been resting on it but his shirt was still pressed straight with sharp creases in it. Before Larry John came along, he used to come by our farm and buy our eggs and corn. He and Mama would argue over the price and when they finally got it all figured out and agreed on, he would still pay extra.

He smiled at us, but his eyes looked tired. "Janey, let me call somebody to watch these kids for you. We need to talk."

"Somebody like who? No good church folk gonna come here at one in the morning." She folded her arms across her chest. "Talk if you need to talk."

"You are not making this easy."

"Nothin's ever easy. Especially not me."

"Right about that." He turned his hat over and over in his big wide hands before he called out. "LeRoy!"

A short policeman opened the door and stuck his round head in. "Yessir?"

Jay leaned over and whispered to me, "When you ever seen a *white* LeRoy?" I had to bite my lip to keep from laughing.

"Please take these kids out front there with you. Give 'em a few of them cookies Brenda made." He motioned to us and we slid out of the hard wood chairs and headed for the door.

White LeRoy held the door open and we both walked under his arm. "Oh, Sheriff? What you want us to do with ol' Doc?"

"What do you mean?" Sheriff's eyes went squinty sharp.

"Kyle and Third are bringing him in the door now. Where do you want us to put him?"

"Why in the blazing hell—" He stopped and put his palms on either side of his head. "Never mind. We'll take him to the morgue soon as I'm done here. No, wait. Call Doctor Marcus and see if he'll come up here and get him."

"Sure, Sheriff." LeRoy patted the top of Jay's head. "Got some dominoes at my desk. You know how to play?"

17

Jay nodded, but he had to be smiling inside. He loved any kinda game from hide and seek to chess. I knew he would beat the pants off the man. Last thing I heard as I closed the door to the meeting room was the Sheriff and Mama talking all serious.

"Do I need to take him to the morgue, Janey?" he whispered.

"Best if you didn't," Mama said.

***

Jay beat white LeRoy for the third time in a row while I sat in a spinning chair and twisted from side to side. My soda was warm, but I sipped at it anyway as I picked at one of the holes in my worn out dress.

Jay's shirt was worn out, too. He didn't have to push up his sleeves to rub at the welt on his arm.

"How'd you get that?" LeRoy asked.

"Bug bite." He didn't even think about it. Musta been working on that one for a while.

LeRoy didn't look like he believed him at first. Then he said, "Looks real ugly."

"Your mama's ugly."

"Yours."

He lifted his skinny little arms over his head in a stretch. "Nope. My mama's pretty."

Officer LeRoy nodded sadly. "Yeah, she sure is." Between the game and the arguing, they were so deep into it neither one of them noticed the coffin move.

It jerked again and made a sound like dragging a stick over a brown paper bag. *Shhhhup.*

I looked over at white LeRoy and Jay, but I didn't say nothing. Just waited. Waited and stroked the crepe wool curls in my pocket.

The soda was keeping me from getting sleepy and the cookies were good too. Soft in the middle, like I like them. I walked over to the empty desk across the room and got another one.

Shhhhup.

"What was that?" Officer LeRoy's eyes ran across the room from corner to corner like a trapped jackrabbit.

"I dunno." Must have been Jay's move, cause he sounded like he didn't care as he studied the tiles on the table.

"That sound. Didn't you hear it?" LeRoy was trying to pick up the trail of something. Felt like he was about to get up and start investigating so I answered.

"Only me getting another cookie." I dragged the tin box across the calendar taped to the desk and it made a soft scraping sound. "Was it that?"

His face didn't quite relax but he went back to the game. "Yeah, maybe."

Jay was staring at me so hard the policeman had to poke him because it was his turn again. He dragged his eyes away, but my brother got the message. It was time to go. Doc was starting to get up.

Part of me wanted to stay and watch, maybe from under one of the desks, but Mama would have a fit. I only saw him wake up once before and it felt like a long time ago. The spanking I got felt like it was yesterday.

Because he was a boy, Jay got to spend more time with Doc when he was brewing. When I cried about it, Doc said spirits and such were drawn to girls that hadn't been with no man before and he couldn't watch out for me and do his work. That's when he gave me the gunny sack doll. She had a faded denim dress like mine and no eyes and black crepe wool hair. I named her Dinah 'cause there's enough "Js" in this family.

Dinah was good company. She sang and told jokes. Sometimes her little red stitched smile would whisper secrets to me in the words Grandma used to use. She knew how Reverend Hollis really paid for his new Cadillac. She told me not to be jealous because Barbara Duncan's beautiful long braids were made of horsehair. When I told her Jay's secret late one night, the little red smile flattened out to a straight line.

"*Dissun ya tok. Gwine da Buzzad.*"

Tears made my eyes burn and I shook my head. "I can't tell Doc. Jay will hate me. I promised not to tell anybody." I held her close, her coarse hair scratching under my chin as I curled up and cried myself to sleep.

But she wouldn't leave me alone. Day and night she talked to me in her thin, crackly voice.

"*E neber ken. Gwine tok.*" Gran's words coming out of cloth and crepe wool. But Gran was gone now and she couldn't fix everything like she used to. And somebody had to do something. So I snuck out after supper and found Doc one evening in the woods where he was digging in the hard packed dirt near a pine tree. And I told him what Larry John did to my brother.

He listened with his fist pushed up against his mouth. Then he sat there at my feet for a while before he said anything. "Your Mama can never know this, you hear? She'd blame herself and she don't need to." Doc scraped deeper into the dirt with an old spoon and pulled another devil's shoestring from the ground and added it to the tiny pile of herbs next to him. "Way back I made a promise to Janey to never work root on this family." He looked in my eyes and I felt the doll stir in my pocket. Crepe wool curled around my fingers. "I'm fixing to break that promise."

The grey in Doc's hair looked like paint smudges as he nodded at Dinah where she wiggled in my pocket. "She tell you to come to me?"

"Yessir." I rubbed my shoe over some pine needles on the ground to make the Christmas smell come out.

"Y'all did the right thing." He looked over his shoulder at the sun dipping low in the sky. "We got a little day left. Help me dig."

I crouched down in the soft, black dirt and started digging with my hands. Even though the day was hot, the dirt still felt cool and moist. It was that kinda dirt Doc told me he had to lie in to work the hex. *Always remember—before you take a man's life, you need to know how the end's gonna feel for him. And you have to accept it. That's the only way God won't punish you.*

I wiped sweat from my forehead with the back of my arm. I already knew to tell Mama when Doc was ready for the coffin, so we could get him inside and she could bury it for a few hours. "Will you show me how to do it?"

I always asked and he always said no. But this time he closed his eyes and just breathed in and out for while. Then he said, "Watch, Jezebel. Be quiet and watch."

Right then, Mama and the Sheriff came out of the meeting room and I stopped remembering.

"If you ain't arresting me, I'm going home."

"Now look, Janey—"

"No, you look here. I got two children 'posed to be in bed by now. I'm done answering questions for tonight." Sweat was shiny on her upper lip when she turned to us. "Let's go, y'all."

21

The door to the police station opened wide and the Dog creeped in.

"Why you letting her go?" Deputy Dog asked, his hand still on the doorknob. "The kids, okay, I understand. But I caught her red-handed."

"Red-handed, with no weapons, no motive and not a mark on the body." Sheriff put his hat on, making him look like a giant cowboy. "No reason this won't keep till tomorrow. Let these kids get some sleep."

"I don't believe this." He started toward us, wild eyed and breathing hard.

White LeRoy stood up, his chubby chest puffed out. "Now, Darryl…"

It didn't help things. Dog knocked Miss Brenda's cookies to the floor with one swipe of his arm and the tin container banged and clanged until it came to a stop next to the coffin on the floor.

"No, it ain't right. I smell something and it sure enough ain't right." He wiggled his finger in the Sheriff's face. "What's wrong, you scared these witches gonna put a mojo on you, huh?"

"That's enough." Sheriff bent over, nose to nose with the deputy. "We will talk about my decision in detail when I get back from the Turner farm. Until then, you need to cool your heels."

He kept an eye on the deputy as he talked to LeRoy. "Did you get Marcus on the phone?"

"No, sir. No answer."

"Better see if you can get over to his place and fetch him to check out ol' Doc. I didn't want to rattle him in the middle of the night, but by the time you get that old coot outta bed and back here, it'll be daybreak."

22

"What about me?" Deputy Dog sounded like a puppy, lost and upset about it.

"You stay here with Doc."

"I ain't staying here alone with him. Where's Third? And Kyle?"

"On patrol. You can radio, but they're probably all the way out past the plantations by now." LeRoy tipped his hat and left.

"Can't imagine what you're worried about, Darryl," Sheriff held his hat to his chest while the corners of his mouth twitched. "What's gonna happen? You said yourself, he's dead."

All three of us followed Sheriff out the door.

Shhhhtuppp.

***

"Fine," Darryl muttered as he stomped over to the coffeepot. The percolator was cold and he cursed as he yanked it free of the cord and went to the small kitchen off the main office to rinse and refill the pot. Most of the men here didn't care one way or another if their coffee was fresh or if it tasted like boiled sewage.

The sound didn't come to him at first, probably overcome by the running water and his sloshing dish soap around the filter to remove all the dead grounds. When the pot was cleaned to his satisfaction, he heard it—a scraping slide like someone dragging a sack of potatoes across a hardwood floor.

He glanced back into the main office of the station, his hands dripping with soapy slush. "Kyle? Third? Y'all back?"

Nothing.

In the next room, the dilapidated air conditioner emitted a whining grind that set his teeth on edge, then settled down into its normal asthmatic hum.

The wind mewled outside and he returned his attention to his task, rinsing his hands and filling the clean pot with water. He wiped the trails of water from the silvery pot and slung the towel over his shoulder. His heavy footsteps stumbled to a halt as he passed the pine box on the floor. "Shoulda left this thing outside. Why the hell would them two fools bring it in here?" Darryl pressed his lips together as soon as he realized he was talking to fill the silence. He gave the box a vicious kick and leapt backward with a shriek trapped in his throat when the lid lifted from the coffin. It settled back slightly askew, but Darryl backed up and strode off to plug in the percolator. He'd take his coffee outside and wait until the boys got back.

As he scooped grounds into the filter basket, he listened. The sound he'd heard earlier was like his scraping of the metal spoon against the metal can. He scooped again and again, convincing himself this was it. But how? He'd not been on night shift in a few weeks, so it may have been that the branches had gotten out of control and scraped the building as the wind tossed them. He'd check on it. These boys wouldn't know what to do without him here.

The next scoop wouldn't fit in the basket and he realized he'd over filled it. He cursed and shook some grounds back out into the tin of dry coffee, not caring about the water droplets clinging to it.

With the coffee brewing, he rolled his shoulders, shrugging off the tightness. He hadn't known being alone in this station would play such tricks on him, that strange scraping being the worst of it. He longed for a drink to settle his stomach, but knew his boss didn't stand for drinking on the job, even on a quiet night. Sheriff had told him about it once when he'd had a belt or two, and he knew he wouldn't get another chance, so the bottle stayed hidden in his desk. He dragged it out now and sat the liter of rye on the desk next to his typewriter. He stared at the amber liquid, rubbing his fingertips over the cool curves of the bottle.

"Shit." He pushed himself away from his desk and headed to the back table.

Darryl poured coffee into a white mug and ignored the brief pain of the first scalding sip. Its bitterness cleared his head of all the strange happenings of the night. That woman had been the start of it. Making his mind go to corn mush. He knew what the darkies said about them Turners—Doc especially—and those were the rumors, the ones of root magic and such, that had his senses off kilter. He leaned his head against the cabinet above the side table where the coffee worked its own daily magic and took in a few humid breaths just as the scraping resumed.

This was crazy, Darryl thought as he turned. Now it sounded like dry skin—

And it was.

Doc's bare feet shuffled across the bare wood floor of the station toward the stunned deputy. Darryl's mouth opened and closed, soundless.

"Must finish," Doc said, his voice raspy. His feet had left a dusty red trail from the pine box as though he'd walked through crushed bricks. He tore the front pocket from the worn work shirt, exposing his concave chest.

The coffee cup crashed down, sending shards of porcelain skittering along the floor. Doc kneeled stiffly, and picked up the handle, using the jagged edge to first slice the base of his thumb, then carefully print a name on the ragged pocket.

Deputy Darryl drew his revolver and held it out in both hands, arms trembling. "You—you are dead, Mister. I-I saw you dead. Fuck, I touched you."

Doc placed the scrap of cotton in his mouth and chewed as Darryl emptied his gun.

***

Mama didn't make us go to school that day. We helped clean up the house. Washed crusty jars and pots. Threw out dried owl bones and scraped wax off tables and walls. When we finally went to bed, I was tired and my fingers and my back hurt. It felt good to lay down, but I couldn't sleep for the noise outside. Jay crawled into bed with me a few minutes later cause he heard it too.

It dragged like a man with a wooden leg. It scratched like nails on a blackboard. It scraped like a stick over a brown paper bag. The sound dug in my ear and made my head feel like a million drums beating all at once inside of me. Even the breeze stopped, holding its breath to see what was gonna happen next.

Doc was home.

***

The next day, the Sheriff and Third drove up to our cabin. I was snapping beans on the front porch steps and Jay was trying his best to catch a chicken as it scooted across the yard. We both stopped as the men came up.

"Where's your Mama?" He asked me.

"Fine, thank you, Sheriff. And yourself?"

Sheriff about growled at me, but Third laughed. "No reason to forget your manners, Boss," he said.

"Mornin', Miss Jezebel." He touched his hat. "Where's your sainted mother?"

I smiled at my little victory. "Inside."

"And where's Doc?"

I grinned even wider. "Inside."

The men knocked on the screen door. Mama shooed us away before she let them in. Me and Jay counted to ten before sneaking back up on the porch and peeking in, one of us on either side of the screen door.

"I need to know what's going on here."

"Just taking some biscuits out of the oven, Sheriff."

Jay looked at me and we both rubbed our bellies.

"Can I offer you one?" Mama continued.

"This is serious, Janey. My deputy is in Carter Rose and we still can't find Larry John."

"Carter Rose? Isn't that the loony place? What's he doing there?"

"Checked himself in. Said with the things he saw, he had to be crazy."

"Oh, my." Mama busied herself at the stove.

"We need to know what happened is all, Miss Janey." Third's deeper voice came around the corner and my face got hot. He was the newest of Sheriff Edwards's officers and the youngest of Mayor Fox's three boys. And he had dimples.

"How would I know?"

The back door creaked open and slammed. "Maybe I can help out," Doc sounded rough, the way he always did when he first woke up. "No reason to bother my sister, Edwards. I am far from dead. You start today with no problems."

"Except for being short a deputy."

"Ahh, yes. Collins, right? But is that really a problem? He didn't seem like the law abiding type, if you know what I mean."

Sheriff's back got stiff. "You gonna tell me what happened in my jail last night?"

"Not much to tell. Seems your deputy passed out and hit his head just as I was getting up. Now, I would have helped him more if I was able. Lying in the cool earth has such restoring powers. Above ground, with this heat, putting myself back together takes a bit more effort." He thanked Mama for the biscuit she placed in front of him and kept right on talking. "Possible he might have caught sight of me before I was decent."

"What about Larry John? Your sister said we needed to talk to him."

"Grown men run away from responsibility all the time. Probably out doing what every other man is out there doing. Trying to survive." Doc chuckled, all warm and delighted as he spread sticky molasses on the biscuit and then licked his thumb. "It's hard for some."

"Think we'll see him again around here?" Sounded like Third had already worked things out. I knew I liked him for some reason.

"I doubt it. Highly doubt it."

"But..." Sheriff said, sounding frustrated.

Doc patted his thick fuzzy beard with a napkin. "You a good man, Sheriff. If you wanted to see Janey, you'd have my blessing."

"I don't need your blessing or no one else's. I do as I please," Mama said as she took off her apron and tossed it on the table. She

28

stomped out of the kitchen with her nose in the air. A moment later, a door slammed.

"Ain't that the truth from the Devil's mouth?" Doc looked over at the taller man. "Janey sure got her ways about her."

"No secret to me, that's for sure." Sheriff looked like he wanted to say something else, but he didn't.

Doc put on his I'll-keep-your-spirit-in-a-jar face. "Larry John is gone from here because I found out he wasn't fit to be around little boys. And I wanted to make good and sure Janey never had to know and feel like she was the cause of it."

"I see."

"Now, you, Sheriff. I'd approve of you seeing Janey." Doc lit his pipe and the smell floated outside, sweet and spicy. "Maybe take her to a picture show. Think on it some."

"I might just do that, Doc."

"Anything else, gentlemen?"

"Not at this time." The men turned to leave.

We scrambled away from the door when we heard the men's footsteps getting closer. The screen swung wide and out came Third, followed by Sheriff. He ducked to get out the door and put on his hat. Third got behind the wheel, but Sheriff Edwards stood there for a time looking up at our house. Then he got in and the car pulled away, up the long trail to the main road, leaving little dust devils behind.

Me and Jay climbed back on the porch and watched the farm go back to normal. Chickens pecked at bugs in the front yard. Mama was back at the stove. Doc's chair creaked off and on.

"Thanks, Jezebel. I was mad at you before, but now..." Jay wouldn't look at me.

I rubbed my hand over his head. It was warm and his short hair felt like the gentle scrape of a cat's tongue on my palm. "I know. Now is different."

We sat there watching the police car disappear, hidden by road dust, until Mama called us in for dinner.

9 Mystery Rose

Gabe gave a long, productive cough, then scrawled an address on a faded receipt and passed it to the man across the table.

Mike cringed and took the paper with two fingers, glancing at it quickly before slipping it into his suit jacket pocket. "Are you sure about this?"

"If there's any help for you, it's there. But I don't know, man." He shook his woolly head like a broken puppet left to dangle without a master. Empty coffee cups sat between the men, ignored.

"So, you think this woman can do it?" He frowned at the diner's laminated menu and tossed it aside. That's what he hated about the South, you couldn't get good food here late at night. In New York, you could get any kind of food, any time of day—get anything, really—if you had the money to pay for it.

"Maybe." Gabe chewed at his cuticles. A strip of dirt lay under his nails. When the waitress refilled his mug, he grasped it with both hands and held the white stoneware against his lips. "So warm."

Gabe had been his link to the seedy side of the tracks when he visited his grandparents each summer, able to get liquor and cars, and girls who didn't know better. In all things shady and south of the Mason-Dixon, Mike trusted him. "Look. If I'm gonna get involved in this kind of thing, it needs to work. And fast."

"I hear you."

"Thing I don't get is how did Karen move all those accounts without me noticing? I wonder if she found out about..."

Gabe grimaced. "You didn't exactly try to hide it." His voice turned wistful. "You had it so good with her."

31

"You don't even understand." The bell on the door tinkled and three squealing teenagers in shorts and flip-flops tumbled into the all-night grease bucket. Mike continued in a hard whisper. "Can this witch—"

"*Mambo*," Gabe corrected, his breath like sour beer.

"What?"

"She is a *mambo*, not a witch. A priestess, a vessel for—"

"Whatever you wanna call her. Can she bring Karen back?"

"I think so. You just have to pay." Gabe pulled the wrinkled coat closer around his thin frame and shivered. "But I dunno how much it will be."

Mike stood and threw a twenty on the Formica tabletop. "Go get yourself some rest, bro. And a shower. You reek."

Back outside, Mike programmed the address into his car's GPS. Gabe's scribbling made the words look as though they read: *9 Mystery Rose.*

"It's 'Road'. Damn drunk." Mike relaxed into the plush interior of the midnight blue coupe as it slid through the half-lit streets. Litter danced macabre steps with the wind in the shadows of the abandoned buildings.

A silhouette darted in front of the car.

"Holy shit!" Mike stood on the brakes. A symphony of screeching tires and florid curses severed the silence. The hunched figure skittered away and faded from view.

Unable to locate address. The guidance system blinked, as if confused.

"Piece of crap. You had it a minute ago." Mike pressed every button on the screen built into the dashboard, but the machine refused to respond. He looked around. No one in sight to ask.

A cloud shifted, leaving the moon exposed and brighter than the flickering streetlights. "There it is."

Number nine crouched at the end of Mystery. A lonely lamp fought to illuminate the shop's front window. Mike parked illegally, on the double yellow lines, sure no cop was anywhere near this place. He hopped out of the car and jogged the few steps to the storefront. He peered inside, and a fluttering movement made him jump back. The door opened and the sweet heat of oranges and chilies wafted onto the balmy air.

He walked into the shop, ducked under the bundles of dried herbs hung upside- down from the ceiling. One wall displayed amber bottles in various sizes, all without labels. A large crow swung on a stand in the corner, its black eye following him as he moved. A single white candle glowed next to the bird and Mike could see his reflection in its unblinking eye. He took a step back toward the entrance.

A nut-brown woman motioned him deeper into the murky room. Her skin, while no longer taut, remained unlined. Two salt-and-pepper plaits escaped from the patterned headscarf wrapped into dizzying spirals around her head.

"What can I do for you, *mon fils?*" She didn't smile as she settled her stooped frame onto a stool next to an antique secretary's desk covered with what looked like sheets of parchment.

"Um, yes. I was told to come here for—" Words failed him when he saw her slice the pad of her thumb and deposit a few drops of blood into a ceramic bowl. This shit was crazy. Even Karen wasn't worth this. "Actually, I'm just looking." Mike slid backward a step. Two.

Her rheumy eyes turned sharp and pinned him like an insect. "Everyone come here for something. You don't find Zéphyrine less you need her."

"My wife died and I was told you could…could…" He swallowed with difficulty. The woman seemed content to wait through his discomfort. "Bring her back to life. I need to talk to her one more time."

Zéphyrine didn't reply, but added a few spindly dried twigs to the blood in the bowl. No other sound moved in the hot shop except the rustling of bird's wings. "Gabriel tell you this?"

Mike nodded, then spoke when the woman frowned. "Yes, ma'am." He pulled his shirt collar away from his neck, then unfastened the top button.

"What else?"

"He said I had to pay you."

"Always payment."

Mike rocked back and forth on his heels while the woman continued to add pungent items from the drawers in the desk to the bowl, heedless of his impatience. Unused to waiting, he tamped down his budding frustration and surveyed the store. A bowl of pomegranates rested on a window ledge, their coarse skins dried and tight. Rolls of parchment similar to the ones on the antique desk were tied with twine and piled seven deep into wine racks. Drawn to the supple finish on a ring box covered in pale, soft leather on a side table, he reached for it.

"Don't touch that."

He yelped and spun around. The mambo, fists on her generous hips, stood toe to toe with him. The top of her head came up to his shoulder.

"How did your wife die?"

"She got sick and—"

"You killed her," the woman interrupted.

Mike's jaw dropped and he looked around him, as if he could locate a camera hidden among rows of incense cones and twirling dreamcatchers. "No, I didn't! Of course not. I loved her."

She flicked her tongue at him. Thick and black, it left the scent of wet ashes on the air. "I can taste your lie." She advanced on him and he banged against the table behind him in an effort to retreat.

A high, weedy screech came from the box as it fell to the stone floor and cracked open. Thin, dark liquid seeped from the damaged corner. "I'm sorry."

"*La verité*, Michael." Her accent deepened; its richness covered him, mesmerized him, lulled his tongue to loosen. "I will hear only the truth."

Mike's vision swam and he swallowed hard, turning away from her searching eyes. "I never could keep a job, but I need money for my lifestyle. Clothes, cars, trips. I was drowning in debt when Karen came along, with her convertible and her trust fund. She spent a fortune on me." His eyes locked with the crow's unblinking gaze. "When we got married, it changed. She put me on an allowance. Said I was burning through her family's money. Said I needed to be a man and get a job and stop bleeding her dry. That set me off."

When the haze of truth lifted, he returned his eyes to Zéphyrine and she was nodding. "How long ago?"

"About three months."

"And you want to know how she hide the money from you? Where it is now? So you don't have to hit a lick at a snake for the rest of your days?" Her skinny plaits wiggled as she shook her head. "I never understand a man don't want to work."

"But I—"

She held up a hand. "Don't matter. Don't care." Zéphyrine went back to the desk and poured the contents of the ceramic mortar into

35

a woven pouch and secured it around her neck. "Payment is due when I do the work."

"You don't care that I killed her?"

"Judgment is not mine. Can you pay?"

What was the going rate for a resurrection? Gabe had said that it had cost him everything he owned, which wasn't much—a few thousand dollars and probably his piece of shit car. Ten thou wouldn't make a dent in Karen's cash. They'd had close to fifteen million the last time he peered over her shoulder at the summary statement from their accountant. He looked around the shop with a careful eye. Although with the state of this place, the witch woman—mango, mambo, who knew?—a couple of grand would be like winning the lottery.

"I'll pay whatever. As long as you're not wanting a pound of my flesh." He quipped, hoping the only Shakespearean reference he knew wouldn't become a portent of his fate.

She didn't share the joke, didn't even react, instead pointing to a dim corner. "I am not in the skin trade. Let us go."

He took the shovel she indicated. There was no sign of the box, save for a smudged trail of dark liquid where it had fallen.

***

Mike followed the old woman as the full moon guided her through the cemetery. She navigated the weary tombstones with grace, making sure her steps never fell on a grave. The moon stopped and hovered over an unmarked section of the well-kept graveyard where the grass had just begun to grow in.

Zéphyrine snorted in disgust. "You didn't buy a stone for her?" A thin metal frame plunged into the ground held a piece of paper with a woman's name written in with black marker.

"I didn't have time. I was waiting until I had the money to do it right." He wouldn't meet her eyes.

"Dig."

Mike took off his suit jacket and rolled up his sleeves. Piles of earth grew higher behind him. His back throbbed, but thoughts of instant financial security drove the shovel deeper. Sweat poured from him. Fine-grained dirt abraded his face and arms. He was aching, ready to stop for a breather when he heard a metallic thud. A few more scrapes of the shovel and he forced the blade of the shovel into the corner of the casket and wedged it open.

Karen lay in the unlined casket, hands folded on top of her prim charcoal suit, her dusky skin ashen. Lank black hair rolled in waves past her shoulders.

Decomposition had yet to eat away all of her serene face, but the skin on her hands had tightened and shrunk them into claws. Zéphyrine leaned in and sprinkled the contents of the pouch onto the body as she murmured in a melodic French. "*Réveille.*"

Karen's eyelids flipped open. A hazy film covered her no-longer-bright eyes, but the orbs rotated in their sockets until they found Mike's cringing form.

Mike pressed against the back of the hole to reassure himself of an escape route. "K-Karen, honey?"

Her jaw opened with a pop and she struggled to sit up. Her right hand caressed her left, then wandered up to smooth her disheveled hair. "Where is…my ring?" Her voice was painful to hear, ragged and unused.

Terror sliced his flesh and crawled in. "I had to sell it. You were gone so fast."

"What...do you...want?"

He thought of what he would do if Karen lunged at him. He could use the shovel. Or if he couldn't get to it in time, he knew his hands fit around her neck.

"The dead do not breathe, Michael." Zéphyrine said, her accented English crisp and dry.

Shit. He turned his attention back to his late wife. "Karen, I miss you. I can't be with you, but I need to ask you a question."

The corpse waited.

"Where did you move our money, baby? I went to settle up some bills and it was gone. Our accounts had barely enough for your funeral." Sweat ran down his face, but he wouldn't wipe it away, in case Karen mistook it for tears.

"I moved it... I thought you were...cheating. Stupid..."

"You know I'd never do that to you."

Karen's face contorted in a rictus smile. "Central Credit...Union. In my...maiden name." She creaked her head to look at Zéphyrine. When she faced her husband again, the smile turned knowing and the wheezing was no more. It was the voice of disdain he'd hated so much that he'd choked it out of her. "Don't worry, my love. We'll be together soon."

Mike slammed the coffin shut. As he clambered out of the dank hole, he could hear Karen's cackling laughter. Free from the hole, he brushed dirt from his slacks and tried to catch his breath. "I'm getting as far away from this freak show as possible."

"There is still the matter of my payment."

"Right. When I get the money tomorrow, you'll get paid."

"Payment is due when I do the work."

"Look, I don't have it right now. You heard her; it's in the bank. But I'll get you your payment, I swear."

"You already have it."

She reached out to him and he knocked her hand away, then pulled out his wallet. "Here's thirty bucks. That's all I've got on me."

The black tongue curled around her thick lips. "I would prefer your eternal servitude."

Mike ran.

Arctic wind shrieked in from behind the witch and tore the scarf from her head, allowing the long, thin braids to crack whip-like in the now frozen air. Icy mist rose from the ground. Zéphyrine's eyes rolled back in her skull, white against the walnut skin as she stretched her bare, fleshy arms to the torn sky. A high, keening cry rose up as the earth lunged and snapped like a rabid dog on a leash. She released its chain. "My legion, the hunt is now."

Mike's dress shoes slipped on the moist dirt he'd se eagerly dug up. He panted and his body dripped cold sweat. He stumbled into another hole, hidden by the cemetery's long grasses, and went down. He clawed at the ground as it retched and split open beneath him. Rot and decay tumbled into his mouth as he tried to scream. He spat, rubbed his tongue on his filth-crusted sleeve.

A skeletal hand closed around his ankle, the flesh on the bone slick with the ooze of decay. Mike stared as the remains of the skeleton pulled itself forward and opened a mouth teeming with bloated maggots.

"So warm," it whispered.

Mike howled and kicked off the thing's grip, scrambled to his feet and fled toward the open cemetery gate. He dodged the grasping hands emerging from the dirt. He risked a glance behind him. They were lumbering toward him, hundreds of them, stinking and leaking putrid gore. He ran harder, trying to outdistance the rotting corpses as they swayed to Zéphyrine's eerie song.

Mike turned to see a milk-white form rise in his path and he could not avoid it. He ran through the spirit and gasped at the achy weakness it left. Hope of escape withered. More hazy forms emanated from the frosty slush, each taking a turn ripping away hunks of his soul. He wobbled, unable to keep his footing.

His steps faltered as the apparitions circled back for another pass, their banshee wails gluttonous and gleeful.

Legs leaden now, Mike sank deeper into the tortured soil. It was getting closer: the rattle of bone, the tattered mutterings… Above it all, the scent of wet ashes. He began to sob.

***

Anthony strolled into the diner and found Mike at a corner table hunched over a cup of steaming coffee. His navy suit jacket was grayed over with dust and his hair stood at odd angles. Mike pushed a thin strip of paper with an address scrawled on it across the table. Anthony looked around before he pocketed it. "Man, you look like hell."

Hand Of Glory

Heat waves always brought out the murderers. And the grip Mother Nature had on Charleston's neck had everyone down for the count. I crushed out my cigarette before entering the interrogation room then rubbed the wine stain lipstick from my fingers. The ancient central air conditioning couldn't keep up with the midday sun and the triple digit temperatures it dragged with it. The room was hotter than Satan's bathwater.

A two-way mirror was the only break in the flat gray walls surrounding the metal table where a suspect slumped, his wrists shackled. The man's eye had a split near the outer corner and while the gash wasn't bleeding, the flesh surrounding it had already begun to darken.

"Tell me it wasn't one of ours that did the shiner," I said to the burly uniformed officer stationed in the corner by the door, his back to a wall.

Officer Butter shrugged. "Don't think so."

"Great," I mumbled to myself. "Just what this case needs." I tucked my white cotton blouse into my trousers then marched over to the table and addressed the man in the chair. "Good afternoon, Mister Byrd. My name is Gloria Jackson, and I'm the lead investigator on the Westbrook case. It's come to my attention you were found with the victim's wallet—"

An eggshell colored blob of mucus landed on the floor at my feet. When I looked up from the splatter, Byrd was grinning at me, spittle clinging to his lower lip. So it was going to be that sort of day. Even better. I straightened my glove and continued where I'd left off.

"—in your possession and copious amounts of her blood were found in your car. I'd like you to tell me something about that."

"Fuck you."

"We have a verbal statement from you, but on listening to it again, I don't believe you've told us everything you know about this matter."

Byrd sucked his teeth as he studied his reflection in the two-way mirror, but was otherwise silent.

His story was he'd picked up Dana Westbrook where she's been hitchhiking off Interstate 26 near Monck's Corner. He said that the girl had told him she was underage—although she didn't look it—so he hadn't tried anything. She was running away from home because her parents didn't get her and she was going to be eighteen in a couple of months anyway.

Byrd had gone on to say the girl was unhurt when he picked her up and was fine when he'd dropped her off at the bus station in North Charleston, some thirty miles away. His explanation for the wallet? She'd left it and her purse under the seat of his car. He even had an explanation for the blood on his passenger seat: it was her menstrual blood. "She was bleedin' like a cut pig," he'd said, laughing. "I wouldn't stick myself in that."

For hours, he's been questioned about her disappearance, but he hadn't said any more. The arresting officers knew it was him…I knew it was him. I needed to find Dana, her parents and the entire city were waiting for news of her whereabouts. They hoped we could find her and bring her home safe.

From the amount of blood and its pattern arcing through the car, I was afraid we should be looking for a body, not for an injured teenager. But if we couldn't get stronger evidence, most preferably Dana, we'd have to cut Byrd loose. I knew that and Byrd knew it too. He'd been on the streets and in the game long enough to know police procedure as well as I did.

"Are you sure you don't want to tell me what you know, Mr. Byrd?"

"I ain't telling you jack squat."

"That's too bad," I said as I sat at the table across from him. "I don't usually brag, but at this moment I have a one hundred percent conviction rate and I'm pretty proud of it. Be a shame to break that streak now, don't you think?" I opened my notebook, braced it with my left hand and scribbled down a few lines.

Disappearance of Dana Westbrook

Statement from Nathaniel Byrd

Nate Byrd frowned at my left hand, the black glove covering it fitting tightly enough for the leather to look shiny and oiled. Then he snorted. "Just one? Who are you, Michael Jackson?"

"Gloria Jackson," I repeated. "No relation, though. Could never get that moonwalk thing down." I clicked the pen closed and placed it next to the notepad. I passed both over to him. "We need your written statement, preferably your confession. Or Officer Butter here can record your verbal confession, if you'd prefer. Whether you believe it or not, I'm here to help you."

"I don't believe a word that comes outta your whore mouth." He jerked on his chains as he attempted to stand up, but they held fast.

Officer Butter stepped forward from the corner of the interrogation room where he'd slouched after bringing Nate in. "Hey, hey! None of that."

He turned his attention to the uniformed officer. "And why not? You boning her? I see." Byrd looked me up and down as much as he was able to with me sitting on the other side of the metal table. "Too much woman for my taste, but the fat girls always have the big tits." He giggled as if I'd tickled him.

43

My lips pinched tight and I knew I looked like my mother had when she'd caught me talking in church. When was that, last week? I nodded at Butter and he slipped his reflective sunglasses out of his shirt pocket and put them on as I gave my final appeal. "This is your last chance to tell me what you know about the disappearance of Miss Dana Westbrook. If you continue to refuse my requests for information—"

Byrd reached out quick as a pickpocket and snatched my pen. Before I could move, he'd brought it down with all of his might— right through my hand. He looked triumphant until he noticed Butter hadn't attempted to stop him or help me and I hadn't screamed.

Also, there was no blood.

"I'm sorry you felt the need to do that, Mr. Byrd." My voice was calm as before, no change in volume or timbre. I wedged the pen out of my left hand by rocking it back and forth with my right until it loosened enough for me to pull out. "Truly is a shame you decided not to cooperate. It would have been easier for both of us."

Byrd swallowed, his eyes on my careful movements as I tugged on each finger of the leather glove, then removed it. I saw the revulsion on his face as my left hand appeared, stiff as a corpse's. The brand new stigmata-like hole through its dry desiccated meat didn't help matters. He tried to scoot his seat backward away from me but his gaze was fixated now. Light emanated from the hand, its gnarled digits cracking as I attempted to straighten the gray, withered flesh.

He moaned as his body twitched almost imperceptibly. Impressive, I thought. Most people can't move even that much when they see the hand.

"Do you know what this does, Mr. Byrd?" His eyes moved frantically left and right—either saying no or looking in vain for an escape. "I'd hoped you wouldn't have to find out."

44

I stood and walked around the table to stand behind him. Try as he might, he was frozen in place, gaze fixated straight ahead where my empty glove lay abandoned on the table. "If you'd revealed your secrets earlier, you may have been spared this. But you've kept them locked up in that little mind of yours. Shut behind a tiny little door. This," I let the weight of my arm lay heavy on his shoulder. "Opens doors."

As I rounded the desk once more, I let my arm slip from his shoulder and I dragged the thick nails of the hand across the table, leaving the tooth-aching noise of scratched metal in the air. Byrd's eyes watered.

"You may not believe me, Mr. Byrd, but I feel sorry for you. I'm told this hurts."

When I heard the soft click of the officer's tape recorder, I placed the hand on Byrd's head.

Hag Ride

Frieda stood in the kitchen's dull light with a chopping knife clutched in one hand. The dinner on the table lay untouched, ice-cold and bathing in congealing fat. Her cinnamon coloring disguised the angry flare of heat in her cheeks. Still, she knew yelling wouldn't get her husband's attention, so she forced a calm tone into her voice.

"Why aren't you staying for dinner? I made your favorite."

"I told you, I got to go out." Henry came out of their bedroom, buttoning up his good shirt and tucking it into slacks she had taken her time to iron that morning.

"Out where? You can't stop to eat dinner with your wife before you go? Give me some of your time?"

"Thought I just gave you some." Henry laughed, his tongue grotesquely pink against his smooth ebony face. He waggled his long, limp penis at her before he tucked it back into his pants.

"Good you put that away. I was going to lop it off."

"You wasn't gonna do that to this valuable piece of merchandise."

"I wanted to spend some time with you. Just us. Like we used to." Tears threatened to fall from her maple syrup colored eyes.

"A man needs some time to hisself, baby. Told you that long time ago."

"I know you did, but…"

He took a pick from his back pocket, a metal one with a balled up fist for a handle and ran it through his short, tight afro. In the hall mirror, he patted it with both palms to even out the 'do.

47

"You never said where you were going," Frieda said.

"Goin' out with the fellas. Relax and get a couple drinks."

"You look mighty nice for a night out with Butch and them." She put the knife down and wiped her hands on her apron. "You promised me no more sleeping around, Henry. Remember that?"

"I know, baby, I know. Don't you worry 'bout nothing." He kissed her cheek and grabbed a pork chop from the platter before heading for the door.

"When are you gonna be home?"

"Late, baby. Real late."

***

Frieda parked the aging Chevy at the edge of the dirt road leading to the marsh. She sat in the driver's seat with the window rolled down and breathed in the sulfurous scent of plough mud and sea grass. Although the marsh teemed with life, loneliness pressed in on her like an unwelcome suitor in the dark.

She walked along the water's edge toward the small house nestled in the marsh's protective embrace, unafraid in the blackness. The moon parted the dark in shifting layers as clouds crept across the Carolina sky. As the toe of her shoe hit the porch, the front door creaked open.

"Evening, Big Mama," she said.

Big Mama stood just over six feet without shoes. Her husky frame held up a massive bosom and her hair, fluffy and cotton white, stood out against her dark skin.

"Lawd, Frieda. You here in the middle of the night? I know what this must be. Get on in here." The Gullah accent, born on the

48

coastal waterways of the Carolinas, was musical as it fell from her dark, unpainted lips.

Cool marsh breeze broke through the muggy night and the thin curtains fluttered. Frieda sat at the rough-hewn table in the middle of what served as the cabin's kitchen and dining room while Big Mama bustled around in cabinets and muttered under her breath. She returned to the table with two jelly jars filled with rose-colored liquid.

"Big Mama, I—"

"Drink this first."

The homemade liquid scorched her throat. She coughed, but the burning cleared her head. The swirling thoughts she'd brought to the cabin solidified into a concrete block of determination. She took another sip of the wine while her godmother eased into the chair opposite and lit a cheroot with a blue-tipped match, producing the sweet scents of tobacco and clove.

"What Henry done now?" The wicker chair creaked as Big Mama settled her bulk into it.

"Same old," Frieda said, turning the jar in her hands, the light from the fire in the nearby iron stove filtering though the glass, causing the liquid inside to shimmer. "Cheating. Staying out all night. I'm tired of it."

"Mmmph." Rings of smoke dissolved in the air.

"I'm married. I shouldn't have to bump around in that house alone all the time."

"That why you got married? To never be alone?" Her snort forced smoke down from her wide nostrils like an enraged bull. "I got news for you, chile. Alone you come in this world and alone you go out. Nothing gone change that."

"I got married because I love him. I just want him to love me back."

"Henry love you in his own way. But that ain't the way you want, huh?"

"I can't live like this," Frieda's whisper hung in the air. "Not anymore."

Her godmother leaned forward and placed a weighty hand on her arm, her scent clean and sweet—peach wine and clothing starch. "You still a beautiful young woman. Find yourself somebody else. Don't let no man be the death of you. Not like your daddy was to your momma."

Tears pricked at the corners of her eyes. "I don't want another man. I made a promise before God and everybody and I will not leave Henry."

Big Mama tapped ashes into a chipped china teacup. "He ain't worth the heartache. You better off alone."

"I don't ever want to be alone again. I hate it."

"Sure it ain't his ding-a-ling you missin'?"

"That's not the problem." She turned away from Big Mama's intense gaze.

"No shame in it, girl. You supposed to like going to bed with your husband. That what make him feel like a man. But it seem your man like going to everybody else bed." A look of sympathy crossed the heavy woman's face and her tone became gentle. "You can't change him, Frieda. You married him that way."

Henry had been late for their wedding. Big Mama and Francis, her fourth husband, had found him drunk in a motel room with a street girl. Only Francis's cool head had kept Big Mama from killing Henry right then. She'd pulled a derringer from her bra and had leveled it at the naked couple. The girl had screamed, the crusty motel sheet held to her nudity, then she'd run for the door.

As the girl passed by, Big Mama grabbed her arm and whispered something in her ear before letting her go hollering out into the sunset. Then she waited while Francis cleaned Henry up and they headed for the church. Frieda and Henry were married an hour later.

"I know I can't change him," Frieda admitted, unraveling the ends of the woven leather belt tied around her waist. "But you can."

Big Mama extinguished the cigar and drained her wine, but said nothing.

Frieda rushed on. "You can fix it so he never strays from me again. You can put him in a jar or something. I've seen you work root. That's why people are scared of you."

Big Mama laughed, the sound a rich singsong echo. "They scared 'cause they think root worse than voodoo. Ain't true. They both dangerous, in the right hand." The chair groaned as Big Mama leaned back and looked at the ceiling of what had once been slave quarters. "Puttin' his spirit in a jar don't stop a man from cattin' no ways. Only one thing can do that."

"The Hag."

"Right. And the Hag ain't nothin' to play with. Not even for me."

"But you can do it."

"Oh, I can do it. But I ain't gonna."

Frieda got up from her chair and knelt beside the woman who'd taken her in after her mother's death and raised like her own daughter. "Please. I don't what else to do."

"What you need to do is leave well enough alone. Find a way to live your life outside of Henry."

51

"I can't. I need him."

"You ain't gonna let this go, huh?" The older woman shook her head and let a sigh escape. "Lawd, that man's thing must jump up and do a dance inside you." She fingered the damp, pulpy end of the cigar. "I can tell you this: if I send the Hag after him ain't no telling what gone happen."

"She'll take that extra energy of his and leave barely enough for me."

"That what supposed to happen. But I just call her. Ain't no way to control her. She do as she please." Big Mama's pause lasted several loping heartbeats before she spoke again. "This ain't for you. Go home. Pray on it. Accept your man for what he is or leave him."

"I can't do that." Desperation grew in Frieda's voice, making it higher pitched than usual. "Why won't you do this for me? Don't you want me to be happy?"

"More'n you know, gal. But sometime you must decide to be happy, even if you ain't. Find a reason."

Frieda picked at her torn and ragged thumbnail. "Do you want me to pay you?"

"Don't talk foolish. My advice is always free."

"There's other rootworkers out there." She kept her tone even and non-threatening.

"So your mind is made up." It wasn't a question.

"Yes, Ma'am."

Big Mama ran her hand through her puffy curls. "When is your woman time?"

"It's here now."

The older woman gaped. "You mean to do this tonight?"

"Yes, Ma'am."

"Mercy, Jesus." The fire sputtered and a length of wood crumbled to ash with a *shoosh*. "No man ever the same after she done with him, you know."

Frieda nodded, not trusting her voice to work around the sudden lump of fear in her throat.

The two women sat on the hardwood floor of the cabin with moonlight illuminating Big Mama's *mis en place* for the ritual. Two piles of rock sea salt, a wad of Henry's coarse hair tied with butcher's twine and six blood smeared candles sat next to the refilled juice glasses.

"This your last chance, Frieda. Think this through."

The younger woman's face remained resolute. "I'm done thinking."

Big Mama nodded and lit the first candle. Murky shadows danced to its flickering. When the final candle began to glow, she spoke. "Get me a hidin' man."

Frieda smoothed her shirtdress and tiptoed out to the marsh, her Keds squishing in the soft, dank mud. The moon was a smile in the darkness as she looked for a stalk of seagrass leaning heavily to the ground. Finding one, she crouched to complete her task, her feet sinking deeper into the cool, black muck. She plucked a conical shell from the crisp grass with two fingers and hurried back inside.

Big Mama placed the open end of the shell against her neck and hummed low in her throat. The hum filled the small room, vibrated across the floor to imbed itself in Frieda's chest and infuse her limbs with its eerie, toneless rumble.

She pulled the shell away from her throat and Frieda saw a small, pale crab, stirred by the vibration, peek out of the shell. Big Mama yanked it from its home and pulled a switchblade, slick with sweat, from the depths of her bosom. In one motion, she opened the

53

knife and skewered the frightened crustacean to the floor before it could scuttle away. Henry's clump of hair covered the crab's death throes. She took a gulp of the caustic wine, spat it on the gruesome pile and touched a candle to it. It flared up, burning bright, but not destroying the wooden floor, while Frieda's voice joined the humming.

Wind came, strong through the curtains and the hovering shadows coalesced into a swirling ash grey mass.

"She here. Be ready with the salt."

The grey cloud moved around the calling space, stopping at each candle, before it slunk between the two women to examine its sacrifice. Satisfied, it slid over to Frieda and swayed like a cobra. She could feel its presence inside her mind, inside her chest and she gasped as it probed at her most tender heartaches. Crushing memories rushed to the surface of her psyche: Henry's countless betrayals, looks of pity from the local women, and laughter from the men. Frieda's heart seized. She gasped for breath as scabs, new and old, tore from each emotional wound. It delved deeper in its search, picking curiously, while tears grew behind Frieda's fluttering eyelids. Her chest heaved and quivered with impending sobs.

"The salt. Throw the salt!" Big Mama yelled, breaking through the creature's trance-inducing sway.

Frieda's arm shook with the effort of tossing a small handful of salt over her left shoulder. While most of the jagged crystals found their way down the front of her dress, enough landed behind her to end the Hag's internal quest. The smoky funnel whirled and spun with its newfound knowledge.

Brought to the surface once again, Frieda's pain solidified into diamond hard resolve, but it eased enough for her to gasp her request before she dissolved into gut clenching sobs. "Make Henry stay with me."

54

The whirlwind roiled with fervor, covering the wine-soaked crab carcass in its dervish. When it finally moved, only the switchblade remained. The coil of ash rose in the thick, muggy air and hovered above the women. One word came from the twisting center eye.

"Agreed."

It extinguished each candle, then dissipated to leave the women surrounded by darkness and the scent of charred sulfur.

***

"Hey, Henry."

"What's happenin', my man?" Henry's palm met his friend's in an intricate succession of slaps before he sat on the next barstool in the smoky lounge.

Butch Dempsey took a sip of scotch and turned a shrewd eye on Henry. "Same old, same old. Working til I die. My life don't change that much."

"I hear that."

"What you doing here, anyway? Ain't this your anniversary night?"

"Shee-it. I was wondering why Frieda was so hell bent on having dinner with me. Shoulda known." Henry ordered a boilermaker from the bartender and rubbed a broad hand over his face. "Damn. How you remember my anniversary and I don't?"

"'Cause y'all got married six years ago on Janey birthday and I never forget Janey birthday."

"Right, right. How she doing?"

55

"Janey? Oh, she has good days and bad days." Ebony circles hung under Butch's eyes, stark against his pockmarked mahogany skin. "Starting to be more bad days. But her mama's with her. Give me a few hours rest."

"I couldn't be sick like that. You know, live my life sick. I wanna go quick. Don't want nobody giving up they life for me." Henry glanced at his friend. "I don't mean nothin' by that, what you do for Janey is good, it's—"

"Yeah, I know." Butch drained his glass and stood. "I better get on home." But he no longer had Henry's attention.

"Uh huh." Henry's gaze was fixed on a woman at the end of the bar. He rose from the barstool, picked up his shot glass and the bottle of beer as though she'd bid him.

"Where'd she come from?" Butch frowned at the sly smile on the strange woman's lips. A chill crept through his bulky frame and gooseflesh grew on his meaty arms.

"Don't know. But I'm gonna find out."

"No, I mean, she wasn't there a minute ago."

"Then she come through the back door." He shook off the hand Butch placed on his shoulder and straightened his collar. "You disturbing my groove."

"You need to stay away from that one. She seems... freaky."

"Just what I'm hoping. Catch you on the flip side, man."

"Henry, wait."

But Henry didn't respond. He had the scent and nothing could get him off the trail.

Butch watched his friend approach the mysterious woman. He started forward to intercept him and the woman looked up, straight into his eyes. Her grey-blue gaze, startling against her tawny skin, held him fast.

All ambient sound from the crowded bar faded. Butch felt himself grow hard and the throbbing ached like a wound. His skin itched like it was covered in dirt. He dug his short nails into his arm with ruthless fervor. Angry welts rose up and still he raked his flesh, unable to get rid of the feeling that she was on him—in him—crawling around.

He yelped when his blunt nails broke skin. The mental hold loosened and he was able to move. Without another glance at Henry, Butch pushed through the throng of people and hurried from the bar.

The woman was chatting with the bartender as Henry strolled up. "Hey man, give the lady here another one of what she drinking." He gave her hourglass figure, draped in a lavender silk jumpsuit, a lingering once-over. "I'm Henry. You sure is foxy."

"And you're a little cocky." Her voice was husky with no trace of Southern drawl.

"You got me all wrong, baby." He took a long pull from his beer then pointed toward her with the bottle. "I'm a big cocky."

She almost choked on a sip of strawberry daiquiri, but it turned into a spurt of laughter. "Now that is one I haven't heard before."

"What's your name, foxy lady?"

"Does it matter? You'll only forget it afterwards."

He leaned closer and her fragrance glided over the smokiness of the bar, a tangy mixture of sea air and citrus fruit. "After what, little mama?"

A coy smile accompanied her words. "After tonight."

"Now, how you know what gonna happen tonight? I might decide to take my time and court you."

57

She shook her head and chestnut ringlets brushed her bare shoulders. "It's my last night in town."

"You got people here?"

"Nope, it's a business trip for me."

"Business? What kinda work you do?"

She ran her tongue over her straight, smooth teeth. "I make people over."

Henry nodded. "That Avon kinda thing? Cool. Cool." He downed the shot of whiskey. "So, this your last night, huh?"

"Umm hmm." She looked up at him, her grey-blues glittering.

"That's a shame. Guess I'm gonna have to work fast." He slapped a ten down on the counter and stood.

"Not too fast, I hope."

***

"You must make some serious bread. This ain't no cheap motel." Henry strolled around the expansive suite, whistling at all the extra touches. Fresh flowers blossomed in a vase on the side table next to an overflowing fruit basket. A corner of the king-sized bed was turned down, revealing crisp sheets.

"I like to be comfortable when I travel." She tossed her clutch purse on the bedside table.

"This ain't just comfortable. This is… nice. Real nice." He stood in the middle of the room, gawking, until the sound of a zipper grabbed his attention. The woman stepped out of the light purple satin puddle at her feet and stood, clad in only a black strapless bra and panties, at the foot of the bed. Any thoughts he might be out of his league evaporated.

"Well, don't stop now." He unbuttoned his own shirt and tossed it on the floor as he strode over to her. She nudged him toward the bed.

"Why don't you lie down and watch the rest?"

"Oh, yeah. I like that, baby."

Henry lay down in the middle of the bed and watched her reach behind her back to unhook her bra. Her high breasts sprang free from their confines and he salivated at the sight of her dark, hard nipples. She climbed onto the foot of the bed and crawled up Henry's body, her eyes laughing with challenge.

She straddled his waist and ground herself against his hardness as she brushed one breast over his lips. He opened his mouth and sucked on the stiffened tip. Warm liquid flowed into his mouth and after his initial surprise, he suckled harder. He tried to reach up and pull her closer, but his body resisted, seizing up with the effort of movement. His eyes widened.

"No, Henry. You don't get to touch me." Her silky voice darkened as her milk soured in his mouth. Lumpy curds drained down his cheeks. He gagged, tried to turn his head and spit, but his thick lips were fused to her slick flesh.

"You asked me what my name was," she said as her fingers stroked his throat, forcing him to swallow the thick pap. Henry groaned as his stomach twisted, but it refused to expel the foul liquid. Her swollen nipple popped from his mouth when she leaned back to remove her brief panties. "It's Eldra." As the silk slid down her thighs, fat drops of her vaginal fluid fell onto the crotch of the panties, bleaching the fabric a sickly yellow-white.

"Don't ring a bell?" Eldra draped the ruined underwear over Henry's face, ignoring his gurgled protests as the caustic fabric burned his skin. "No one here calls me that. They call me a hag. Can you believe it?" She slid down to his crotch, her bristly pubic hair like needles in his groin as her nails ripped through denim and exposed the length of him. She squatted, legs wide, her nether lips open to expose two tiny rows of glinting silver-white teeth.

His scream bubbled through the lumps in his throat as she lowered herself onto his stiff penis. Eldra shoved her fingers into Henry's open mouth, turning the panties into a putrid gag as she rode him with demonic wildness while he lay immobile, unable to stop the flesh-rending fuck.

Hours later, Eldra climbed off his limp, wasted body. She gave an impressed grunt. "Ooh, Henry. You're still hard." She took his mutilated penis in her palms and gripped it, holding the flayed pieces together. Her salt and citrus scent filled the room as she lowered her acidic mouth again and again.

***

"We patched him up the best we could, Miz Frieda." The young nurse said as she reached for the door to the shared patient room at Saint Francis Hospital.

Frieda blocked the door with one outstretched arm and whispered, "How bad is it? I mean, how is he?"

The nurse hesitated. "It's... uh... He's been asking for you."

"Frieda? That you?" Henry's voice was high-pitched and weak. "Frieda, please. I need you."

He sounds exhausted. That witch must have done her job.

"I'll be at the desk if you need anything." The nurse made a hasty exit.

60

Frieda hovered in the doorway, twisting the knob back and forth. The police had found him in an alley, the doctor had said, unconscious. He'd been beaten badly, but his clothes were still neat and pressed, as if they'd been removed and replaced later. They'd wanted to talk to her more, but she said she needed to see Henry first. She put iron in her spine and pulled the door open and strode in. Two beds were inside—the near one cradled an old man and the other housed a hunched figure, turned to face the far window, covered in a thin blanket. No sign of her husband.

She walked toward the window until she heard a rasping voice behind her. "I'm here. Frieda. Here."

Slowly, she turned to face the first bed. Her breath caught in her throat as she realized it was her husband, her Henry, small and shriveled in the middle of the bleach white sheets. His face was a mass of blotches, where his formerly smooth dark skin seemed to have dissolved. At the corner of his lips, white chunky crusts formed. *I need him,* she'd said. *Now look at him.*

He reached out a shaky hand to her, his flesh slack over the wasted muscle. One of his eyes was wide and pleading, the other a cloudy grey. She stepped toward the bed and pulled back the sheet covering his lower body. *No, not that, too.* Shriveled to nothing, the fragile skin was held together with tiny black stitches.

What you gonna do now, Frieda?

Two officers waited for her in the hall just outside the patient room, she could see their indigo uniforms through the window. One of them looked up and met her gaze. Absently, she patted Henry's hand then beckoned the men to enter.

"We'd like to ask you some questions, Mister Cannon. Are you feeling up to talking about what happened to you?"

Henry turned his head into the pillow.

"Henry," Frieda whispered loud enough for both men to hear and nudged his arm. "Answer them."

When he didn't respond, Frieda closed her eyes and her hand dropped away from her husband's shoulder. "Officers, I don't think he's up to talking to anyone right now. Maybe you can come back in a little while. I'm going to get some coffee."

All three of them left the room and headed toward the canteen. The taller man placed his hand at the small of her back to usher her forward and it sent a thrill through her where it pooled into her core. She looked up into his disarming grey-blue eyes. "It's gonna be okay, ma'am."

Frieda knew that it would.

Homegoing

"Everything in life you told me not to do, I done."

It was the saddest thing my son had ever said to me. And the scariest. But this was his way of getting back at me, removing the blame from himself and placing it on my shoulders.

Don't know how long I sat there silent, thinking about why he said it until I felt his eyes on me, wide and waiting. He wanted my reaction, I realized as I regarded him through the prison's visiting room Plexiglas barrier, scuffed with the remains of so many other fights before ours.

"Like what?" I asked.

"No, Mama!" His tone made me jump and I scolded myself for being so nervous. So scared of my little boy's voice, full to bursting with anger and desperation. "You're supposed to ask me *why*."

"Oh," I said. "Why?" Only now did I realize how obedient I could be to my son, but not to my husband or my vows. I sat there in my best church hat, marveling.

He sat back in his chair, hair buzzed almost bald, revealing his pale scalp. A faint raised scar shaped like a sickle marked where he'd been hit with a beer bottle five years before. It was a fight over some worthless girl. That's how he'd known, he'd told the papers. When he fought over some girl and she'd still walked away with the loser he'd beaten to a pulp that he'd vowed never to care about another woman. To make them all pay.

Upon seeing the scar, his M.O. solidified in my mind. Jesus take the wheel. I was thinking like one of those TV shows now. Modus operandi. Method of operation.

I'd felt lightheaded in the courtroom when the prosecutor described it. Out of body, I floated above the pictures of my son's handiwork. I was beyond the words of the medical examiner. *Wounds consistent with a curved blade. A lot of force. Brutal force.* The cutting words of the prosecuting attorney yanked me from my daze with just as much viciousness.

Severed heads, their scalps always found yards away from the rest of the body. The defendant's semen dried into their long hair. Eight young women, the prosecutor had said, his Armani suit tailored to his lean frame. He looked at the jury over the top of his trendy yuppie glasses. All under twenty-five. I'd fainted.

A guard appeared in the door behind my son. "Phillips, five minutes left."

Now, I shook my head and asked again. "Why?"

"Cause you let me," he picked at his teeth, then looked at his finger. "You always let me do anything I wanted."

So it's my fault? I wanted to scream at him and storm out. Then I'd never need to have another body search in order to visit this festering hole south of Hades. Never have to endure another seedy, depraved look from the men on the inside, their sweat rank with the stench of captivity.

Men really did devolve without women. I stood and left without another word, my legs and back stiff and wooden. Sweat ran down the middle of my back under my suit and into the waistband of my pantyhose. When I got into my car, I turned the air conditioner to maximum. Pray for him, Lord just make it okay. I didn't see any of the road the entire drive home.

When I opened the door, the rich meaty smell of roasted chicken hit my nose and my stomach roiled. Hat carefully placed on the hall table, I greeted my husband. "Visit went all right today."

"Um hm." Bill's head was buried in the Sunday paper, likely the food section. His roasted chicken was the best I'd ever tasted, but right now acid bubbled up my throat and threatened the back of my tongue.

My hands shook as I removed my suit jacket and hung it over the back of a chair, content to stand in the living room in my bra and camisole, letting the icy air chill my damp skin. "He looks okay, just thinner. When he finally comes home—"

Bill interrupted me, his tone one not to argue with. "He's not coming home, Agnes."

"He's our son." Even to me, the words sounded weak as water.

"He's a murderer. A serial killer." He threw down the paper and ran a hand through his thinning hair. "God, all those girls... It makes me sick."

"One day he'll get out. I prayed to get the verdict overturned. He didn't do all of that...that what they said he did." The room swam and I grabbed the back of the chair to steady myself. "There's a chance he can still get out."

"Not as long as I'm here, there's not."

My heart tripped, fell into nothingness. My voice was a stage whisper as I repeated the words that had been my mantra all through the investigation and the trial. "He's our son. We raised him."

"Well we fucked up, didn't we?" Bill stood up from his recliner, grabbed his jacket from the peg in the hallway and stormed out the door.

I ran after him to the garage door, my stocking feet slipping on the polished hardwood. "Where are you going?"

He didn't answer. Just got in his car and drove away. Some men would have peeled out, screeching tires and stinking smoke. But Bill buckled his seat belt and checked his mirrors before reversing out into the cul-de-sac and away. And he didn't come home until five hours later. When he did, he wouldn't let me pull him into conversation again.

After that so-called argument, Bill never discussed Hardin prison again. If he had—or at least come to see his son once—maybe I wouldn't have let that guard escort me to my car. And I definitely wouldn't have listened to him when he said he didn't live far away. Maybe then his offer of coffee and a sympathetic ear would have gone unanswered.

But I stayed, against my better judgment. In the guard's bed and in my son's corner. My next two months of visits to Hardin tumbled by in a blur. Today wouldn't be so kind.

"You know something? My baby isn't going to be anything like me."

"Your what?" Heat rushed to my face and my heartbeat sounded loud in my chest, like hail on a rooftop.

My son ran his hand over the peach fuzz on his face. "My wife is having a baby. Oh, yeah. And I got married. Didn't I tell you? It's the only way you can get a fuck in here. From a chick anyway."

Heat boiled over inside me. How did they let him marry? Who would marry a man convicted of murdering eight women?

I stuttered, but no coherent words came out. My shock and dismay brought a smile to my son's face. "I'll tell you more about it next time. I gotta go. It's con-jew-gull visit day."

He pushed back his chair with a scrape that set my teeth on edge and strutted out of the room, his oversized orange jumpsuit baggy around his waist and hips. As the guard ushered him out, he winked at me over his shoulder.

I walked out of the visitation rooms in a daze, my short steps almost heel to toe. All around me, the prison flashed by as if in fast-forward. The movie reel in my mind of my son growing up was the only normal thing. Holding him for the first time. Teaching

66

him to swim. Clapping and whistling at his championship soccer game. At the front desk, I fished around in my handbag for my keys.

A young woman approached the desk where I stood and handed the attendant a box wrapped in bright paper. When she gave her name as Mrs. Phillips, I turned to look at her squarely.

Thin and not fashionably so. Her eyes had a dull look, sunken and vacant. Resigned. Desperate. But it was her hair that made me snap. Long, lank blonde hair.

"He did it you, know. He killed them," I could hear my voice rising, becoming hysterical. "What are you doing here? Why are you visiting him?"

The girl shrugged, unsurprised by my outburst. "Why are you?" Her dead tone gave me a start, which quickly turned to itchy fear, but somewhere deep inside, I felt the need to defend myself.

"Because I'm his…" The word caught on my tongue and I bit it back. I didn't want to speak it aloud. Didn't want to claim him or his deeds. But I was tied to this monster, had held him in my arms for years, inside of me for months and still the need to deny him burned deep.

Before I could cough the word out, the girl turned away. Then she followed the guard through the sliding iron bars, leaving me on the outside.

I knew it with a certainty that hadn't been there before. All of the support and faith ebbed from me as I walked to my car. False hope giving way to a resignation that was somehow freeing. There would be no celebration. My son wasn't coming home, ever. And now, finally, I didn't want him to.

Empty of spirit, I drove. For miles. Ended up at a hole in the wall fish shack on the outskirts of the city on the way out to Edisto Island. I hadn't been down this way since I married Bill and we set up life in suburbia. The scent of frying peanut oil drew me inside and I dusted the seat near the door with a napkin before settling into it.

Not many people were there—Sundays were days to eat at home with family, if you had it—so the young woman behind the counter wasn't delayed in sauntering over to my table. She looked me over with heavy-lidded eyes. The crack of her chewing gum was like gunfire. "Yes, ma'am?"

I had no idea why I was here. I didn't want to go home to face an end to my devotion. What would life be like if I just let my son go? No more visits, no asking the congregation to pray for him. How do I give up on him? "What's the special?" I let my Geechee show, ending consonants smeared to nothing and vowels stretched to their limits.

If she was surprised, the waitress didn't show it. "Whiting platter. Fried or baked. Two sides. Dinner roll."

My son's favorite. I hadn't fried fish for him since he was a child. Too messy. Too much grease. The smell clung to the curtains and the couch and the carpet and it wouldn't come out. Only time faded the smell, not the aggressive effort of cleaners and air fresheners.

"Two fried platters to go."

The meals were ready in minutes, packed up with plasticware and a surplus of napkins. When I got home, the bag was still searing hot and I removed it carefully from the floor of the car.

"I'm so sorry to be late." My apology to Bill I'd worked out in the car—I was hours late and I hadn't called. It was so unlike me. I'd tell him the truth about the baby and say I'd needed time to myself to get a handle on a new addition to the family. "But I picked up dinner. I hope you didn't cook…"

Bill sat at the dining room table, head in his hands, cordless phone on top of the folded newspaper. No smells wafted from the kitchen. I placed the bag on the table and lowered myself into the chair across from him.

"What is it?" The strength in my voice surprised me.

"He's gone."

I didn't need to ask who. "When? How? I was just there."

"A few hours ago. Poison." He shook his head. "From a cake some young woman brought to him. Where does a girl get cyanide?" Bill raised his eyes to me and I saw my emotion reflected. Pain, confusion and relief. "They said it was some kind of a wedding cake. Did he—"

"He said he did, but I didn't know before today. And I don't know when it happened." I plucked at the plastic tie on the bag. "What about the girl?" God answers prayer.

"They shared a slice of the cake. He's at the morgue. We're supposed to go down there."

"We will." I opened the bag and pulled out the Styrofoam containers of fried fish, potato salad and spicy collard greens, their scents entwining to make a soup of fragrance that would, in time, fade. "After dinner."

With the Turn of a Key

For the third time that day, James thought about drowning himself. He stood in front of his custom-built beachfront home on Daniel Island and didn't want to go inside to its artificial coldness. Instead, he leaned against the hood of his car and closed his eyes. Salty breeze dampened his thinning hair and caressed his face. Ocean waves, with their rhythmic Zen-like lapping, called to him with promises he was finding harder and harder to resist.

He knew he would be able to rest beneath the endless sea. It would be the sanctuary he couldn't find here on land. With his fortieth birthday now behind him, James felt he was beyond the spontaneous carefree acts of youth; adulthood came with a sense of commitment and duty. He'd made choices he would have to live with for the rest of his life. He shrugged off the thought of watery bliss and went inside.

A strange key waited on the dining room table with packing paper strewn all around the cherrywood surface. He picked it up. The length of his palm, it was light for its size. The shining surface suggested a metallic composition, but the key seemed to float in his outstretched palm.

When he examined it more closely, he saw a pattern of engraved vines on the key's head formed a dense curtain. The surface felt damp, but his hand stayed dry. Why was it here? Surely such a thing belonged to another place, another time. He looked at the brown envelope where it rested and saw it was addressed to him: James L. Chamberlain.

"James! Is that you?" A shrill voice came from the other end of the house.

"I'm in the dining room." His heart leapt in his chest, then finally settled into an erratic thundering as he waited for his wife to join him.

Stacy stood in the open doorway that connected the kitchen and dining room. "Who is that from?" Her tone was iced with a thick layer of suspicion.

"You opened my mail?"

"I'm your wife."

"But that doesn't—"

"Who is it from?" She crossed her arms over her surgically enhanced chest and her lips tightened in disapproval. Her severe ponytail made her eyes appear large and penetrating.

"I don't know. There was no return address. What did the delivery man say?"

"It was in front of the door when I got back from the doctor." She tried to frown in spite of the skin tightening treatments. "Don't pretend you don't know anything about this. Nobody would send you a key without a note unless you already knew what it opened."

He shrugged his shoulders, rounded from countless hours hunched over paperwork and keyboards. "I have no idea, Stacy."

"Right. You sure it isn't the key to some tramp's private estate? You could try to be more discreet." Her smirk drew first blood.

"You know what?" Years of frustration made his temper flare. "I'm tired of working my ass off six days a week and not getting any appreciation for it. Not even a hug and kiss at the end of the day. Maybe a tramp on the side is exactly what I need. I could keep her on retainer."

The smirk softened into a placating half smile. "Goodness, honey. I was just teasing. You know I appreciate you." She gave his shoulder an awkward pat before she trotted upstairs.

He trudged up after her, to his own room, too tired to ask about dinner or what else she'd done with herself all day.

They hadn't shared a bedroom in almost a year, not since he'd pressed the issue of having a child. Neither her tears nor her halfhearted attempts to seduce him into forgetfulness would distract him. This time, he'd persisted. His persistence had brought to life a monster.

Her face had twisted into a grim parody of itself and her voice had leapt an octave. It was her body, she'd screamed. She'd just started to lose weight, she'd argued, now he wanted her to be fat and miserable for nine months. In the background, he could hear frightened seagulls take flight, their wings flapping like miniature sails in the wind.

When his mother was alive, he might have sought her counsel. It had been just the two of them growing up and she had always listened to his problems when he'd exhausted his own solutions. He could see her in her cane-backed rocking chair, nodding as he spilled his guts, keeping the motion of the rocker going with one bare foot. But she would have shrugged her well-padded shoulders and continued to crochet. *That's what them white girls is like, darlin'.* Then she'd pat his hand and give him a gentle, gap-toothed smile. *You'll do the right thing, baby.*

At Stacy's insistence, he'd moved into one of the house's other bedrooms. She'd said she needed time and would invite him back when she was ready. The invitation never came. All attempts to coax Stacy into talking about a resolution to their situation fell flat. James wished he was one of those men who would break down a door and take her—ravish her, they called it in those so called romance books she read endlessly—make it so good she couldn't help but give it up. Instead, he threw himself further into his work, desperate to be successful at something concrete.

His libido, so long suppressed, became little more than a pleasant memory. He clutched the key in his fist. This wasn't what

73

he wanted out of life. He had a lot to offer the right woman. Maybe it would be worth losing half of everything he'd worked for to get a new start.

His eyes burned with fatigue and an insistent pounding started above his right temple. He lay the key on his nightstand, shed his clothes, and fell into bed.

***

James woke, rested and content, nestled next to a shape, curved and warm. He stirred and the shape twisted to fit the contours of his body for the span of a breath before it retreated. He groaned at the loss of contact and opened his eyes.

A woman stood at the foot of the king-sized bed, her lushness swathed in a luminous material that seemed to move of its own accord. Around the span of her hips, the fabric gleamed foamy white. His gaze was drawn to her weighty breasts supported by a black-green drape, the color of the ocean at midnight. He couldn't see her face, but he knew she was looking at him.

Waiting.

He stood and took the delicate hand she offered and her touch was tender and cool. In one step, they were transported to a winding stone path that led to a city in the distance. They spoke on the way, his mouth moving, hers not. He already loved her smiling lips with their perfect Cupid's bow the color of a ripe pear: pale green blushed with rose.

The stone city, when they reached it, glittered in welcome with its haunting, aqueous glow. Algae covered columns and statues shone as if crusted with diamonds. He followed her to a coral gate, where she pulled a key from her bosom. *The* key. His heart thudded, pushed against his chest, strained toward her. She fit it to the ornate lock and it swung open. He'd walked her home. A wave of adolescent heat filled his body.

The woman came to him, reached up to pull his face down to hers. Crisp, the taste of her. Damp and fresh. His hands trembled as they stole around her waist. James closed his eyes as her fingertips fluttered over him, twined in his hair, stroked his face. When they traced the shell of his ear, he shuddered.

She slid from his arms, took his hand, and led him to the gate. He hesitated for a heartbeat, afraid to step through, and found himself standing at the gate, alone.

***

James woke again, this time in his own bed. Sunlight streamed into the window and he knew he'd overslept. Deep relaxation oozed from every cell in his body and made the curiosity he felt over the faint red circles on his face and chest little more than a passing thought. In his rush to shower and dress, he neglected to notice the key on his nightstand, where it lay in a puddle of brackish water.

He came home late that night to an empty house. Stacy's voicemail said she'd had too much wine and was spending the night at a girlfriend's house. The ambient chuckling whispers floating through the line gave him doubts. He heated tomato soup in the microwave and drank it from the bowl. He felt as though weights were tied to his limbs when he ascended the stairs.

In the shower, thoughts of the dream from the night before returned. The hot pelting water eased his strained muscles and the swirling steam brought the remembrance of the mysterious green woman's silken hands on his skin. He braced his own hands on the wall of the shower and lowered his head to allow the pounding water to beat on his neck and back.

What if he had walked through that coral gate? He didn't know the woman at all. How could he have followed her into what might have been nothingness?

He soaped his exhausted body and rubbed some of the foam into his hair. What did time matter? He had known Stacy for three years before he proposed. Twelve years later, they spoke only when necessary and money passed between them more often than laughter. On the occasions she did embrace him, the contact was brief and left his heart emptier than before.

James dropped into bed. Why was he questioning what he did in a dream? That showed level of stress his life had taken on. He was unable to make a decision even when the outcome didn't matter. He rarely had dreams. Sheer exhaustion usually kept his sleep deep and undisturbed. But he knew dreams were supposed to be manifestations of the subconscious mind as it brought to the fore issues it wasn't able to resolve during waking hours. He needed to resolve this thing with Stacy. He needed to cut back on his working hours. He needed to eat better. So much needed to change.

You worry too much, baby. His mother's words echoed in his mind as clearly as if she'd said them a moment ago. He took the key from the table and turned it over in his hands. When presented with the choice the next time, he would go for it. Grasp at the chance to be happy even if it was only for a few blissful hours in the dead of night. His eyes were heavy and for a moment, his lids lowered. The lamplight slid across the key's surface like oil. It was then he noticed the picture again. The network of vines on the key's head had parted to reveal an image of the gate to the stone city. It meant… something. His lids lowered again and he fell asleep, the key clutched in his hand.

***

James stood in front of the coral gate, but his mystery woman was nowhere in sight. This time, he knew he would have to come to her. He used the key and the gate swung silently open.

The streets of the city were empty, but the entire place vibrated with unseen life. James walked slowly, listened for her voice inside his mind, but there was only an otherworldly silence, like he was sitting alone at the bottom of a pool. He called to her, using endearments and love words, since she had never told him her name. He felt a touch of shame for not having asked anything about her.

His gaze darted from side to side, in hopes of catching any sign of movement, a signal to where she might be. A glint caught his eye. An obelisk stood in the middle of the city, unknown symbols carved into one side of the rock. He approached the stone tower with confusion. How was he to know this language?

James studied them carefully, but the signs meant nothing. He resolved to search every cavern, every doorway in this city until doomsday—until he found her and his life became complete. Thoughts of her burned away all else. Resigned, he trailed his hand over the face of the stone as he began to leave.

The rock warmed under his palm and its intermittent glinting grew into a full viridescent glow, which turned toward the south like the beam from a lighthouse and illuminated a silhouette in the distance.

He ran down the lit path toward the figure.

She stood at the end of the path, dressed this time in rolling waves of blue. Still he could only see her form up to her full lips.

"Show yourself to me," he said.

I am here.

"All of you."

The blushing pear lips smiled and the dreamlike haze lifted from her face.

He came to her with gentle kisses. Tender and searing. He stroked the fine, poreless skin of her neck, trailed his fingers along her collarbone. His mind tumbled over the edge of sanity, lost to him. The ache inside him was heavy, throbbing and pulsing with its own life, its own need. But he suppressed it for her.

But she would have none of his restraint. She took his hand and in one breath, they stood in front of her bed. His fingers found, then loosened the braided tentacles of her hair and they came to fervent life, stroking and caressing his face and neck with a maddening suction. He lowered her to the bed, as he tasted her briny lips again and again.

"You love me don't you?"

Always, she said.

It was only later that she asked James if he wanted to stay with her.

"Where? Inside this dream?" His smile was broad, born of bone deep satisfaction. "It's perfect here."

If you wish to call it that.

"You're my dream," he said and reached for her, but she evaded his grasp and repeated her question.

His limbs heavy with sleep, he nodded. She placed her delicate pale green hand on his chest, over his heart, then gave a brief, sharp nod, seemingly pleased with what she found. *Your heart belongs to me.*

James could not deny it.

The woman smiled, and slid her leg over his, situating her body upright on top of his prone one. James groaned as she lowered herself onto him, sheathing him in a pulsing grip. She rode him firmly, head thrown back. He watched her rhythmic gyrations, holding his groans back as best he could until he saw the ceiling above them change.

Solid white faded into cloudy, swirling whorls of water. The woman panted in her exertions as the churning water thickened into a maelstrom, her tentacled hair waving wildly. For a moment, the storm cleared and James saw his house, his bedroom, saw Stacy as if he lay on the floor of a clear lake and looked skyward. He gaped at the sight of his lover's tentacled hair growing longer and thicker before the stalks shot upward, out of the dream and into his life. He struggled to right himself, to sit up and do something—anything—but her grip was too strong.

Hush, my love. I've almost...got it. There...

James screamed.

***

Stacy returned home the next morning, sated and more than a little sore. She was careful to remove the satisfied smile from her face. That radiant afterglow? She planned to tell James she'd been to the gym and had doubled her workout. The words to her story prepared, she walked into the house.

She grabbed a bottle of water from the fridge and took a long gulp before wiping her fingerprint smudges off the stainless steel.

"Hey, James, I'm home."

In the dining room, she glanced through the mail and found nothing but coupons and other junk. "James?"

Silence answered her. James's car was in the garage. She went upstairs, yelling his name every few steps. All of his clothes were in the guest bedroom closet. His bed looked slept in. Stacy jogged back downstairs to look for the note he must have left. The kitchen and the dining room tables were bare. Her cell phone had no voice or text messages and James knew she hated e-mail. Her calls to his office went directly to his answering service. Where was he?

Her heart jumped and began to rattle her ribcage like an angry prisoner. She opened the French doors and stepped onto the deck and scanned the beach for her husband. She expected to find him as she sometimes did, staring out over the ocean, his lanky frame stooped against the chill of the early morning wind. In one direction, the sun rose on an elderly couple as they walked hand in hand at the water's edge, smiling at the children as they squealed and ran from the incoming waves. In the other, a man jogged with his dog, both of their tongues lolling out. No James.

The clicking of her sandals echoed as she crossed the marble kitchen floor. She climbed the stairs again, unsure of herself for the first time in recent memory. Stacy pressed a few buttons on her cell phone and waited to hear James's voice. Her puffy lips twisted. No matter how plausible his explanation, she wouldn't accept his bumbling apologies. Then she'd leave an issue of Harper's Bazaar open to the jewelry section on the dining room table. When the box arrived, all would be forgiven.

A faint, familiar buzzing sounded in the quiet house. She followed it to the guest bedroom where James slept. His phone, still in its holster, beeped and vibrated on the en suite bathroom counter. Stacy hung up, confused. She picked up a squat bottle made of thick glass from the countertop. The cologne smelled like autumn wind, fresh and cool and crisp. Alone in the empty bathroom, surrounded by the scent of her husband, she trembled.

A glint from the bed caught her eye. She perched on the edge of the comforter and placed her palm against the rumpled sheets. They were soaked and the sun shone off what felt like flecks of sand. If James had walked on the beach and gotten into bed wet and gritty, she was going to—

The bed beneath her began to rock and sway. The pillowy surface of the mattress darkened and sloshed like the ocean in a windstorm. Her feet came up off the floor as her bottom sank into frigid water. She screeched and flailed her arms, windmill fashion, to gain enough forward momentum to break free of the roiling waves.

The bed was now a whirling dervish of foamy sea. Stacy fell forward with a grunt of effort and a gasp of pain as her hip struck the hardwood floor. On her hands and knees, she crawled toward the bedroom door, icy water dripping from her clothes. Her hands slid out from under her in opposite directions and her chin hit the polished floor with a crack. She lay there, moaning, until she heard a sound that made her scramble with renewed vigor.

It was the sound a hand makes when it slaps the surface of a pool. The sound a body makes, curled into a cannonball, striking the water. The sound of something from the bed searching for her. She scurried across the floor as quietly as she could manage. She reached for the door handle and winced at the loud scrape of her heavy jeweled bracelet.

Alerted to her position, a tentacle shot out from the bed and coiled around her legs. She twisted onto her back and tried to kick free, but the grasping appendage tightened its hold. She looked in horror at the undulating mass of pale green tentacles as it rose from the center of her husband's bed. She screamed when the aquatic limbs stretched toward her, the tough webbing that connected them spread open like a gaping maw. A cold tentacle snaked around her waist. Her terrified wail was cut off by the dripping slap of another limb across her mouth. Suckers constricted around her jaw until she heard a resounding crunch. Then red, searing pain.

The frigid tentacles dragged the struggling body away from the door, further and further from escape. Dragged it along the wet floor, up over the footboard and down, down to its final rest beneath the frothing waves of the sea.

Devil's Playground

Night is the time when
Yellow Sun becomes Blood Moon
Evil comes to play

Darkness hosts the game
Tree branches like dried fingers
Indicate the starting line

There are no time outs
While you live you must join in
Last hope for this race

Come! Sit in the swing
When he pushes your back, feel
Breath full of cold heat

Leap off and tumble
Run and hide He is counting
The time you have left

Cold hands Touch of ice
He has found you Game over
Until tomorrow…

Path of the War Chief

1655 - Fifteen years before the establishment of the
English colony of Charles Towne, along the banks of
the Combahee River in what is now Beaufort, South
Carolina, the home of various indigenous tribes
descended from Mvskoke Indians

Aponi stood at the edge of the settlement and watched her life-
mate walk away toward the salt marshes, knowing she would never
see him again. Or if she did cross paths with Chief Tyee, neither of
them would know it.

During the Eagle ceremony to protect the kin-tribe, all of the
men danced around a blazing bonfire, their arms and heads draped
in white feathers. Black clay covered their eyes, raccoon-like, to
show their lack of knowledge of things to come, their leaps and
spins in time to the frantic drumming filling the village.

Most of the women sat in a wide circle around the men. They
were clothed in fine beaded dresses, their sleek braids wrapped in
bright cloth as they sang, shaking gourds filled with dried beans to
accompany the dancers. A few of the women, Aponi among them,
stood outside the circle at its edge, away from the others. These
women wore their hair loose, restrained only by the chips of bone
and shells woven into their tresses. Their voices did not join the
song.

Tyee had given his name at the calling place in the middle of the
sweat-laced dancers, and since there was no visible opposition from
He-Who-Never-Dies, the Chief left with a promise to return with
the one thing that would prevent a war between the lands. She'd
seen the determination and fearlessness in her life-mate's black

eyes and knew death would find him quickly. The urge to cry out a warning rose up, but it stuck in her throat like a dried husk and she swallowed it down with effort. Inside she felt full of holes, dug up, hollowed out.

So it is with Those-who-see.

She stood on the soft ground, head straight and back proud. Even at her age, her skin was dewy and unlined, except for that on her feet. That skin was tough and held a grayish cast, but once Tyee departed it did not stop the other men's glances from being full of open curiosity.

Aponi watched until the winds erased the Chief's footsteps before she blinked away the thick smoke of burning sage and white oak and gathered her moccasins from the pile. She walked toward home, the sounds of the Dance behind her throbbing in her ears as she placed one small bearskin boot in front of the other to make the journey longer.

Haparak, her sight sister, joined her. "Be glad you have a son," she said, her hair lashing her face like whips. "He will live in ignorance and be happy for it."

The sight sisters continued the walk in silence, because it is one thing to know another's pain. Quite another to speak it. Haparak was in mourning herself, her mate having died of fever a season before. She had removed her eyebrows with boiled sweetroot, as was the custom, and it gave her eyes a desperate, pleading look. Her hair fell to her shoulders, straight and black.

Aponi's blood held more of the dark Ancestors and her mane rolled down her back in deep waves like the night sea, although now those waves were streaked with grey. They each counted their steps until they passed out of the main village.

Only one sight sister Aponi knew of went mad. Before Aponi was born, it was said Nahmana had tried to put an end to her gift by removing her own eyes. But her sacrifice did nothing save increase her powers. Without the distraction of real eyes, her sight reached far, far into the world. Nothing past or future was beyond her. The People said she had lost what-was-real. The old woman told crazy stories and spoke to invisible persons. None ventured near her without fear.

Nahmana sat in the darkness outside her hut made of hewn logs and thatched palmetto leaves. On the ground in front of her, a friendly fire crackled. Her thin body shivered despite a thick covering of furs and hides. Firelight baked her skin while she swayed, entranced by voices only she could hear, her chants and moans so much rhythmic nonsense.

"Do you want me to stay with you?" Haparak asked, her long crane-like body already poised for flight.

"No, wait for me in my hut. I will not be long."

Relieved, her Sister squeezed her shoulder and scurried off.

Aponi approached the edge of the hut and kneeled, silently asking permission to join her elder. Despite what she told Haparak, she was prepared to kneel until the day rose from its slumber. But the old woman waved her over, her song approaching its climax. Her wrinkled lids were shut, but as the song faded, she opened them to reveal dark, empty spaces the light did not reach.

"Wounds," the old woman said in a voice like the crunching of long-dead bone. "Deep. Running red." Her hands looked almost youthful as they fluttered around her craggy face. "Taste thunder and live."

"Grandmother," Aponi addressed her with respect, her hands open and relaxed, palms up, receptive to whatever the woman might say to help guide her decision.

Instead of responding, Nahmana pulled an egg-shaped vial made of earthen pottery from beneath her robes and removed the rubber tree cork with a flourish. From the jar, she extracted a short stick and flung her whitened hair back. Two fat drops of liquid fell into each empty eye cavity. Aponi watched, horrified, as dark moisture slid down the old woman's cheeks and gathered under her nose. It ran like the Combahee after a thaw. Her tongue came out, a long red thing, and licked away the drainage. Aponi shuddered.

"Have you tasted thunder?" Nahmana asked. "First it burns, then it drips sweet onto your tongue. And the knowing leaves. For a little while."

Aponi didn't answer. She had already pushed herself to her feet when the old woman spoke again, stopping her.

"Is the path dark to you? Yes. You cannot see yourself. Should you follow your foolish man?" She tilted her head and leaned forward as though listening to a secret. Then she giggled. "Or should you wait for war to come?"

Nahmana's body shook as though the Ancestors had walked on her grave. "Or is there another way? Take the drunken path. It weaves this way and that, calling to you with the promise of lies. There you will find an answer."

Brother Fire was dying and neither woman attempted to save him. The old woman's lids drooped and she mumbled nonsense again, all coherence lost to her. On hands and knees, she crawled into her hut and tucked the thatched flap closed.

Aponi rose from the fire, her knees crying for relief. Where the wild woman once sat, the egg jar lay on the ground, catching the last flickers of light. The letters painted on it were not of the Mvskoke. Even the jar itself seemed out of place, its pale color unusual. The clay the women made here was from red mud and held a rusty hue once baked.

Over the years, their tribe had welcomed all others into the walled village with arms open. They had shared their ways of building huts, fishing, and making cheeses from deer milk. Taught them how to grow pumpkin and melon and how speak the language of the saltmarsh. Even spoke of what it is to see without eyes. And what had that achieved? It had brought them to the brink of war.

Aponi looked down at the container, no longer than her first finger and she kicked it away. The jar slid across the black dirt, hit the edge of the log doorway and ricocheted off. It spun and rolled and came to rest against her booted foot.

The war chief's wife stared at the hut, where slow, even breathing now emerged. Without thinking further, she scooped up the jar of thunder and left for home.

Haparak was waiting for Aponi when she returned and she placed a cup of sweetgrass tea, fragrant with honey and herbs in Aponi's hands.

"Can you gather the sisters at first light? We must visit the elders," Aponi said.

"I have already asked," Haparak replied.

**

Sun was slinking into the sky when the sisters of the kin-tribe gathered outside the large square council house of elders. Aponi knelt at the wide opening with Haparak at her side.

"Tyee is dead and the People need a new chief."

Faces softened by time looked at the each of the sisters in turn. Aponi believed that to the old ones they seemed like a group of wild animals, manes flying in the breeze, shell and bone clicking like hooves. "You have seen this?" The eldest among them, the old chief, spoke.

"It is seen and known." The sisters answered as one.

When he nodded in acknowledgement, Aponi said, "I place my feet in his steps."

There was only the sound of fire in the square as the elders passed the pipe. Each one drew deeply of the heady green earth-scented smoke. Two rounds of the circle were complete before the old chief spoke again. "You are a woman. A woman has never led the People during war."

"What of Godasiyo?" Haparak spoke, barely keeping the irritation from her voice. "It is said that for a time we were once all together under her laws."

"A legend only." He refilled the pipe and puffed again. "What of your son?"

"Sixteen winters is not enough when the scent of war is so strong." Aponi gazed into the fire, her head filling with visions heightened by the rich tobacco smoke. She closed her eyes. "His head is still in the wind and he heeds no words but his own."

Grunts of agreement preceded the words the women knew would come. "We will wait, sisters; the Spirits will bring the answer to us."

Haparak opened her mouth to speak again, but her sister stopped her with a hand on her arm. To the elders Aponi said, "I understand and accept your wisdom."

They departed the square silent, leaving only the sound of hooves fading into distance.

Back in her hut, Aponi spoke freely to the sisters about the meeting with the elders. To Haparak she said, "I give you this task, most trusted of women."

Haparak did not respond and kept her eyes turned away while she pulled the soft deer skins close around her thin body.

With a sigh, Aponi continued. "Tell the others where I have gone."

Tears gathered in Haparak's pleading, desperate eyes. "Where *are* you going?"

"To walk the path as I was told."

Haparak's eyes widened, but she remained silent, rivers streaming down her bronze cheeks as she embraced the older woman.

"I am only doing what I must. Do not be afraid of what you see for my journey."

"No, it is not that," Haparak said. "I am afraid because I can see nothing."

***

Day was still sleeping and cool dewy mist lay upon the early morning air when Aponi followed the path her mate had taken seven moons before. She walked and walked, watching the morning rise above the treetops. When Yellow Sun was high atop the trees, the path before her split into three. She had come from the south and a path curved off in each of the other directions.

East, trees and bushes grew thick and dense, covering most of the muddy footpath with low-hanging branches. Along the West path, rocks the size of bear heads rolled along a dry dust road alongside tiny pebbles. The North path was clear. It could not be the one Tyee took. Too smooth and simple. Aponi turned East.

On the East path Aponi had to crouch and crawl to keep true. She followed it as best she could, pushing away scratchy bug-filled moss and snapping apart the sweet smelling wisteria vines in her way. The path continued until the trees disappeared behind her and the blue-gray of the sea beckoned. Her knees ached and her feet were hot and sore. More than anything, she longed to remove her boots and cool her feet in the rolling waters. But she held her pack tight against her chest and skirted quickly as she could down the shore path, determined to reach its end before taking a rest.

But no.

Aponi realized she was back at the crossroads where she started. Confused, she looked down each path again as far as she could see. Then she closed her eyes and opened her mind, to allow the sight to bring what knowledge it pleased.

But there was no answer.

Her head began to beat like the drums from the Dance. Soon, she reasoned, White Sun would be chasing Yellow Sun from the sky and all would be dark. She decided to rest and begin again at first light.

But night never came. She rested under the shade of one of the East's dense trees. Aponi, weary and frustrated, drank from her water skin as she stared at the West path. This must be the way Tyee went. Movement came from a thin bush lining the North path and her hand went to her knife belt. A small rabbit came from the bush and sat in the middle of the clearing. She watched it watch her, its nose and ears moving as though it wished to speak. To her astonishment, the rabbit's mouth opened and a screech filled her ears.

A red hawk swept in, clutched the frightened animal in its claws, and flew off with its meal. Droplets of blood lay on the dirt where it once stood. She covered her mouth as she watched the bird rise into the warming air, circling up, up, with the limp, furry body.

"Does it disturb you, Sister?" The mocking voice was close to her ear, the words hot and moist, and she jumped. "The true and honest taking of life?"

A man, younger than she, leaned against one of the large rocks between the North and West paths. He was dressed for hunting in deerskin shirt and breeches. His face was narrow, his nose long and beak-like, his lips thin. Of the People, but somehow not.

"No, Brother, it is only that…" She trailed off, considering her words. "I did not see it in my mind before it happened."

He laughed, a cackling sound. "You are lost."

"The paths twist and tie together and I cannot understand them. The other path—"

"Has already brought death," he finished. "A bad omen." The man cocked his head, observing her. In the shade of the boar hog tree, his eyes were a solid black.

Doubt and confusion warred within her and for the first time, she was unsure of what to do. "I am lost," she admitted.

A sly smile crossed his face. "Not the words of a chief. A true leader would walk the drunken path in silence."

"Then that is where I must go. Where is the drunken path?"

"Why should I tell you?"

She had no answer.

"How do you even know of it?" He asked without inflection.

"Nahmana told me it is so."

The cackle grew into hooting laughter. "That old one still lives? I would have thought her food for the earth long ago." His laughter slowly died and he turned solemn and thoughtful. "I think…she took something from me once. But I cannot remember."

Aponi took her turn to watch the strange man. "How do I know it is not you that is lost?"

"Perhaps." He stepped out from the tree toward her. "But I am not so lost that I do not know that one foot on that path," he pointed West. "Brings an end to you quickly."

"Who are you?" Aponi asked, not giving ground.

The man's eyes widened with surprise, until white surrounded the dark. The dark spots trembled and shook. Then he frowned. "I am the Guardian of the Path."

Aponi looked West. The rocks, piles of them, rolled along the dirt and faded dry grass. As she watched, she saw faces appear in the stones. Images of those who had passed from this life into the next. They groaned as they made their progress back and forth on the road, tumbling over each other. Grinding each other to powder as more rocks emerged from the burial mound and tumbled down to join the melee.

When she returned her gaze to the stranger, he was watching her. "If you are nimble, you may make it down to the end. But you must not touch the stones or let the stones touch you. Do not speak to them or they will follow you." He smiled with darkness. "Go quick. Quick."

Aponi knew the time of her blooming was past. Cold lingered long in her bones now and fleet of foot was not her way any longer. "I do not care if the stones follow me."

"No? Do you not see them? The faces that you know? Perhaps you want to give your life for one of theirs." He shrugged. "Pluck up a stone and it will take over your body and your face will replace its image in the rock."

She gasped, more with shock than fright. "I have never heard anything like this."

The stranger scoffed, his wide nostrils flaring. "Do you think you know all there is under the sky? Then you have already proven yourself a fool."

Her own anger rose. "A fool is one thing I am not. I did not come here for this insult."

"Then why did you come here? To this place outside of your own?" The wind stopped as he spoke, quieting at his now soft voice. Heat from the full sun blazed down on both of them, scorching Aponi's bare arms and making her shield her eyes. He did not react.

The question removed her guard. She'd acted on instinct, guided by Nahmana's cryptic challenge. Her mouth opened, then closed again without a sound.

"Silence?" He mocked. "No need for words, Sister. I know why you are here."

"Why?" Her voice was dry, thick in her mouth and she had to force the question out.

"Because," he said, walking in a slow, wide circle around her. "You want to wear the feathers of the hawk. You want to lead the People."

"How do you know that?"

"It is the only way anyone can arrive here, where the Earth's roads cross." He stood in front of her now, searching her eyes. "And there is only one way to become Chief."

Aponi crossed her arms in front of her body. "One way?" She prompted.

"Yes," he said. "To wrestle." At her look of horror, he continued. "If you are able to pin me to the ground, you succeed and I will guide you on the drunken path."

"And if I do not succeed?"

"Then you will join the stones."

"But I am a woman. And past my youth. How can I triumph over one as large and strong as you?" Aponi bit her lip after her outburst, ashamed she had voiced fear that she, as she was now, might not be enough.

"As Chief, you will not always have the advantage. But yet you must face the enemy." The unsettling smile returned. "I wait for your choice."

After a few deep breaths, he received it. "I accept."

He removed his shirt. "Good. Good."

Aponi ducked from the man, pushing away his brawny arms as he tried to take hold of her and toss her to the ground. If she could avoid his grasp, she might be able to think of... something. But he was like a bear and a coyote as one animal, strength dancing with speed. With ease, he took her knife from her belt and tossed it away before she could think to use it.

Her mind raced and another thread of fear ensnared her. Already, she was tired from her sudden movements and he laughed, performing fancy tumbles between swipes at her thighs and feet. What was her advantage? Neither the grinding of the stones on the packed earth nor the beat of the waves against the land brought answers. Desperate for those answers and without her sight, she listened to their songs a heartbeat too long and the man caught her.

His long fingers twined in her hair, making the clack of dried bone loud to her ears. He brought her in close to his chest, his heartbeat becoming hers. His smell was different—higher and colder than the soft, marshy damp of her People.

"Who are you?" Aponi asked again, breathless from exertion. "Who are your People?"

"You have lost." He kicked at her knees and they buckled, bringing her swiftly to the hard ground.

Now he had her legs pinned beneath her and she was unable to free herself. Her fists only made him laugh at her struggle.

"Do you give in? You have no weapon against me. I have won."

Her mind whirled like the winds and for a moment, she heard Nahmana's voice. "I cannot hear you," she said to the stranger.

"I have won." His voice caused the rocks to cry out and the sea howled.

Against the pain, she shook her head. With one hand, she touched her ear. "What did you say?" With the other hand, she reached into the small pouch sewn into her hide jacket. As he drew in breath, her hand closed around the egg jar and she pressed her thumb against the gum rubber tree bark, uncapping it.

He leaned into her face and yelled loud enough to shake the shells from her hair. "Do you give in?"

"No!" She threw the thunder in his face, the liquid catching him full in the eyes. His screech brought the winds rushing from all directions, tearing trees from the ground and grinding the rocks to meal. Dirt and dust fell around them. He rolled on the ground, curling into himself like a baby and rubbed at his eyes, calling out with frantic words she did not know.

Aponi climbed atop his prone body, planting her full weight on his chest so he could not pull in another deep breath. She covered her head to protect it from the falling stones and branches and soon, all was quiet. She lifted her face and the man was lying underneath her, his eyes clear and calm. Shaken and a bit embarrassed, she stood from her crouch with care.

"You have returned me to myself, child." He too, stood. "Now I will take you down the path you desired to go." Aponi stared as his body moved like oil during the change. His arms grew long and wide, crossing far down the path roads. Light and dark feathers covered him.

She climbed on his back and he flew above the drunken path. Far North, she spied a hunched figure in the marsh grass. Her guide circled, then dipped low to the ground for her to wrap Tyee's body in her blanket and pull it from the marsh's sucking grasp before they took to the sky again toward the kin-tribe.

The People were gathering for war, the world full of cries and arrows. All this stopped as the Thunderbird landed in their midst with Aponi on his back. She slid off and the great bird bent for her to remove her husband's torn body.

"You have my thanks, Aponi." As the tribes looked on, his body changed back to that of the man at the crossroads of the drunken path, but the great wings remained. He removed one of his feathers and wound it into her hair. "May your people serve you and heed your wisdom for many seasons." He leapt into the air, winds carrying him until he was no larger than a hawk in the sky. A clap of thunder sounded and he was gone.

Aponi crossed to the circle of elders and kneeled, palms turned up. Her wait was not long as the old chief shuffled to his feet and came to stand before her. As he placed a trembling hand on her head to give his blessing, rain began to fall.

Since Hatchet Was a Hammer

Sandra found it curious that there was a hatchet under the bed in the guest room of her mother's new condo. She'd found it after she'd placed her luggage in the corner and lifted the floral print dust ruffle covering the ironwork bed frame.

"Uh, Mom?" she asked. "Did you know there's an axe under the bed?" She heard her mother bustling about in the next room as well as a seventy-year-old can. A seventy-year-old who bowled a 163 game.

"Oh… yes, just leave it. It's fine where it is."

"Yeah, but why is it here?"

"You never know what you'll find when you move, sweet pea. There's all kinds of things in this place." Her mother had moved into the condo overlooking the Ashley River less than a year ago, not long after her father had died. The family house had become too much for her to manage and the two-bedroom condo fit her need for reduced square footage and fewer memories.

To Sandra's surprise, her mother had bought it without asking for her input on the purchase. She'd been her mother's consultant on these things since Dad took ill almost five years ago. But when her mother told her everything was completed and she could visit whenever she wanted, Sandra had been stunned.

"Miss Maggie told me about this place and when I saw it, it just felt right," she'd told Sandra on the phone one evening. When Dad had first died, her mother had called her nightly, nervous about being alone in that big house with all of its creaks and groans. Robert, on night duty, hadn't been around to eavesdrop on her calls, so she'd been able to speak freely.

"You mean that crazy lady from the shelter?" Her mother was afraid to talk to no one in the city, and she'd frequently found that by talking with a person long enough, they had some sort of connection—be it blood or otherwise.

"Hush all that. She's no more crazy than you or me. Just had a hard time for a while, that's all. And that can happen to anybody. You wouldn't know her now. She looks good."

"That's good, Ma." She settled into her favorite armchair with a package of frozen peas to ease the ache on her right side—Robert was right handed. "So, tell me about this new place."

"It's safe, that's the biggest thing. You know, protected."

"It's gated? Or there's security?"

"That too. There's a twenty-four hour caretaker on site as well."

"That's nice, Ma. Let me know if you need any help moving."

Her mother paused, then took a breath to say something. Sandra froze, not sure what she'd say if her mother came right out and asked if Robert was abusing her. It wasn't like her; her mother was more the type to draw conclusions from her own personal observations. During her marriage to Robert, Sandra had gotten to the point of imagining the worst-case scenarios in all of her dealings with people. But her mother only said, "You too, darling girl. I'll call you tomorrow night, okay?"

Sandra looked forward to their talks, more than she'd thought she would. A deep part of her wanted to spill everything: the fights, the beatings, the threats, but Sandra couldn't burden her mother with the horrors of her own making—not at her mother's age.

Each night they talked, reminiscing and sharing gentle gossip, until her mother had moved into the new condo. After that the calls had slowly dropped off to a comfortable weekly call. Then Robert had hit her in the face.

She couldn't recall the trumped up reason why—maybe she hadn't been responsive in bed or she'd forgotten to give him his wallet when she'd removed it from his jeans on laundry day—but it had knocked something loose inside of her. Knocked it into place, was more likely. When he'd left for work, Sandra had packed her things and jumped in the car.

She walked around the condo, admiring the efficient floor plan. The two bedrooms were on opposite sides of the home, giving each inhabitant needed privacy. The guest bedroom shared a door with the main bathroom, which was off the hallway leading from the front door.

"I love your new place, Mom."

Mrs. Case smiled her thanks. "If you're scared you can sleep with me tonight."

Tempting as the offer of mother comfort was, Sandra was looking forward to sleeping alone. It seemed a privilege to sleep sprawled in the middle of the bed. Not worrying about disturbing anyone or having to duck punches. "Not tonight, I don't think. After that drive, I'm going to crash."

Sandra found it more curious that the hatchet was no longer under the bed in the guest room of her mother's new condo when she went to sleep.

***

"Mom, this place is so perfect." Sandra sipped her coffee, rich with real cream and a spoonful of raw sugar. "The right size, the right location. No offense, but I'm surprised you could afford it on what you got for the house." The economy was in the gutter and even property wasn't the best investment.

"I got really lucky. This unit had been sitting vacant for ages. It was a bargain." Her mother came out of her bedroom in a purple nylon tracksuit and navy bowling shoes.

Sandra pursed her lips, but held her tongue. "There's a noise like pipes creaking in the wall. Doesn't that drive you crazy?"

"It did at first, but now I'm used to it. I can almost predict it."

Strange. Her mother was usually a nitpicker over things like that. "What exactly is it?"

"Some type of machinery the caretaker uses, a chipper or something. The sound of it is quite...comforting." Mrs. Case poured her coffee—black with one artificial sweetener—into an insulated travel mug. "I'm going bowling. You want to come along or are you going to be okay?"

"I'll be okay here." Her mother kissed her cheek and she winced as her lips brushed over the yellowing bruise on her cheek, covered with thick pancake makeup.

"I should stay home with you."

"No, it's fine. Have fun, Mom." Sandra hugged her and felt the thinness of her frame under the voluminous tracksuit. "We'll go out for dinner later." After her mother left, Sandra realized she hadn't felt this relaxed in years. The time with Robert had changed her, made her edgy and jumpy. She sipped the sugary brew and flicked through the satellite channels. Her cell phone rang and her body jerked, sending coffee sloshing over her hand and down her arm. So much for losing her nervousness. She looked at the screen before she answered.

"Hello?"

"Are you okay?" Her friend Jennifer's voice trembled within its whisper.

"Yeah, I think so." Sandra went to the buffet cabinet and opened the bottom right drawer. Not everything about her mother had changed. She poured a healthy slug of dark rum into her cup. "I should have told you before I got in the car, but I—"

"No. Don't tell me anything. Then I won't have to lie." Jenn drew in a shaky breath and rattled off the next words without pausing. "I called to tell you that I overheard Mike on the phone. Robert just took a week's vacation time from work." Sandra heard ice clink in her friend's glass and the glug of thick liquid. "Gotta go. Be careful, girl. Love you." Jennifer hung up.

Sandra's hand shook as she refilled the coffee mug then went back to the dining room table. A ray of sunlight came through the ancient oak trees and she reveled in its heat, soaking it up in an attempt to break the chill encasing her. She was still in the same seat when her mother returned from the bowling alley. "What'd you do today? You're still in your pjs."

"A friend called me today."

"Oh, that's nice. Who?"

"She said Robert took a week off from work, starting today."

"Mercy, Lord." Her mother sat her pocketbook down on the table and rummaged in it. She found her keys and twirled them in her fingers.

"I'm just trying to…I don't know what I'm trying to do, Ma. This place is gated and I thought—"

"Do you think he's coming here? How would he know where I live?"

Sandra stood from the chair and paced. "I mean, he can't be, right? But he's with the police. He could look up property records. You had to file the house sale, didn't you?"

Her mother wrapped her arms around her. They felt strong, but softer than she remembered, her skin looser and more delicate. "Don't worry, baby. This condo complex is secure. You have to have a key fob to get in the building." She showed Sandra the grey plastic tab, elliptical shaped and no longer than her thumb, as she turned it in her fingers, pressing and smoothing it like a worry stone. "We're safe."

Mrs. Case ran a hot bath and Sandra gratefully stepped into peach blossom scented bubbles. As she soaked, she heard her mother singing in the next room, her falsetto soprano familiar enough to lull her into a semblance of a doze. When the water had cooled and the bubbles had died, Sandra roused herself to climb from the deep tub. There was no more singing, but her mother was talking in her bedroom. It was whispered sound, but as she crept closer on her bare feet, she was able to pick out select words—enough to determine it was a conversation, not her own mutterings.

"Four years."

"Too much."

"For good?"

The floorboard in front of her mother's room creaked and the whispers stopped. When Sandra, wrapped in an old fleece robe, came padding into the room her mother was alone and sitting on her bed, remote control in hand. The curtain at the window fluttered.

"Mom, the air conditioner's on, why is the window open?"

"Sometimes I like fresh air. It can get stuffy in this place."

She sat next to her mother on the bed. "Who were you talking to?"

"Talking to? Nobody."

"I heard voices in here. A moment before I walked in."

Her mother smiled the same way she had when Sandra was in grade school. The smile that was supposed to reassure her that the other kids teased because they liked her but didn't know how to express it. "Just the TV."

Sandra looked at the TV, its screen flickering with images, but no sound. The white curtain lifted, floating on the cooling night air. She crossed to the window and looked out, her fingers running over the sheer fabric. Nothing below moved.

"How come someone in this family is always in some mess?"

Her mother gave the same answer she always had. "We're the Cases."

"This was the right decision," Sandra said, pulling back from the window and closing it. "Coming here."

"I'm glad, baby."

***

Sandra was finishing her jog as the sun crawled into the sky and the streetlights flickered off. She'd run an additional half hour, her heels pounding on the pavement, trying to get the past twenty-four hours out of her mind. As she rounded the path to her mother's building a man stepped out from one of the patios.

"Robert," she struggled for breath. "How did you find me? What are you doing here?" She wanted to run, but her legs were gelatin, wobbly and soft. Her energy was near gone—she didn't eat before a run—and she'd saved enough to get back to the condo and fall into bed. Fatigue settled in her chest like bags of sand buffering against a hurricane.

Robert ran a hand over his bald head. "I'm just here to talk, Sandie."

She hated that name now. It was the one he used when he brought home an extra steak for her black eye.

"I don't want to talk," she said. Instead of assertive, her voice came out breathy, winded.

"You sound so sexy, panting like that." He stepped toward her, arms outstretched. "You can get me all sweaty if you want." His grin was part mischievous boy, part feral wolf.

"No, I don't think so." The street was quiet, but the day was already warm. Barely dawn, the sun hadn't completely chased the night away. No one was around as the community was mainly older retired residents, no one had to get kids on buses or beat the eight o' clock traffic.

"This is stupid, Sandra. You're the one who left me, but I'm apologizing."

"You've never apologized to me. Not once. It was always my fault for getting you angry or moving your keys." Her outburst took more of the wind out of her and she sagged against the column in front of the building entrance. "I don't want to live like that anymore. Always wondering what's going to set you off, because it changes every time. I can't keep up."

"It'll be different, I promise. You know my job is stressful. When I come home and the house isn't straight and food isn't cooked, it makes me a little crazy." He jiggled his keys in the pocket of his jeans. A quick glance around told Sandra his car wasn't nearby. Or he had a rental.

"I could've handled things better." This was Robert's standard line, an acknowledgement, never an expression of remorse. "Come home."

Sandra wiped sweat from her eyes, they were stinging and the dogwood tree-lined parking lot was starting to blur. "No, not this time. I want out."

A visible darkness passed over his face. "You ungrateful bitch." He grabbed her arm, lightning quick, and yanked her to him, ignoring her squeak of protest. "I came home to you every night. Do you know how many women throw themselves at me on a daily basis? To get out of tickets or not go to jail?" He tightened his hand around her wrist and Sandra could feel the bones grind together. "And what do I come home to? To a cold oven and a colder bed."

She pulled at her arm, but he held it fast. He raised his other hand.

Headlights came on across the parking lot, illuminating the pair, and an engine started, making them both jump. Robert dropped her wrist and walked away as if he'd only been passing by. "Run, Sandie, run." His taunts faded under the sound of an engine coming to life. She watched the Shaded Arches truck pull out of the parking space and turn in the direction her husband had taken.

Her mother was in the kitchen stirring a pot when Sandra stumbled in. The scent of microwaved bacon filled the steamy room as Mrs. Case filled two bowls with creamy white grits and dotted each with butter.

"What happened to you?"

"I just saw Robert," Sandra wheezed and sank into one of the bar chairs, all of her adrenaline spent.

"How did he know you were here?"

"I don't know, Mamma." She didn't have the energy to remind her mother about their earlier conversation, the house sale records, any of it. "I don't know anything."

"Call the police."

"And say what? That I left my husband in Virginia, he came down here to find me and wanted to talk?"

"No, say he's been beating on you since hatchet was a hammer and you can't take it no more."

Sandra stared at her mother, speechless.

Mrs. Case sat next to her daughter and answered her unvoiced question. "A mother always knows. Not sure how, but we always do."

She lay her head on her mother's shoulder and inhaled her gentle scent, gardenias and Tide. They sat in silence until Sandra finally spoke. "You got that from Gramma, didn't you? I remember her saying it. Exactly how long has a hatchet been a hammer?"

"As long as anyone can remember. Since forever. Now, let's go get breakfast instead." Mrs. Case took off her track jacket to reveal a "Sexy Senior" t-shirt.

Sandra winced. "Ugh. How about we stay here forever?"

"I know what you mean, love, but that never solves anything, does it? You gotta go on living your life." She looked at her daughter and pulled her reading glasses from her nose, letting them dangle from the beaded chain around her neck. "What are you going to do now?"

"I...I'm not sure, Mom. I feel like I messed up so bad this time that I can't ever make it right." A sob welled up in her throat, born of shame and embarrassment at having made the wrong choices, and she choked it back with effort. Her parents had made so many sacrifices for her over the years, working extra hours to send her to private school and driving her all over the city for various music recitals and plays she'd been in. They'd driven up to Virginia to help her move into her first apartment. That all seemed like so long ago. "I think I ruined my life," she whispered.

Mrs. Case hugged her daughter close, then pulled back and damp tendrils of hair away from Sandra's face, where they'd begun to curl. "No life is ever ruined until it's all over. That's when you have no changes left. You can recover from this. You'll see."

A light knock sounded at the door. "Don't answer," she pleaded with her mom. "Look through the peephole. It might be him."

"Relax, honey. Must be Miss Maggie from upstairs. She said she'd come by this morning to bring me some article from the paper she wanted me to see." Mrs. Case winked at her daughter. "We old ladies need to check on each other, especially when our kids live so far away."

Instead of the elderly neighbor, Robert stood at the door. He took advantage of her mother's shock and elbowed his way past her and into the condo.

"You can't come in here. I don't want—" Mrs. Case's protests were cut off as Sandra's husband shoved her away from him— hard. She fell against the guest bathroom door and it yawned open. Sandra screeched as she heard her mother emit a cry of alarm, followed by a crack against the ceramic tiles and she started toward her. Upon seeing the rage in her husband's face, she stopped short, then scurried away to hide behind the couch.

Robert made a beeline for his runaway wife as she tried to hide behind the sofa. "Did you think I wouldn't find you? That I didn't know you'd run off to *Mommy*?" He dragged the couch away from the wall and sneered as he dragged Sandra from her hiding place by her ponytail. "How did I find where she lives? Easy. House sales are public record, available to anyone that gives a shit. I didn't even have to leave my desk to find out where you were. Where else would you go? You're not the type to make it on your own."

Sandra wailed until he slapped her, the pain halting her cries for a moment. He released her hair and she slumped to the floor. He grabbed her face, his thumb and fingers pressing into her jawbone and forcing her mouth open. "You got some nerve, bitch. Who do you think you are, huh? My wife. Mine!" Spittle flew into her face and she closed her eyes.

Robert tossed her away from him and she hit the wall, back first, and all of the air whooshed out of her lungs. Her high school graduation picture wobbled on its hook before crashing to the floor next to her. Sandra tried to pull in a breath, tried to get to her feet and stand, but she couldn't move. She stared up at her husband as he marched toward her, reaching her side in three long strides.

Sandra could only watch as he reached down and hauled her up to her feet and higher, higher, until he pressed her against the wall of the condo with his hand around her neck. Her wind was back, but she knew better than to use it to cry out for help. Who would come? Instead, she could try to reason with him or keep silent.

She dragged her now rough tongue over her dry lips. "Robert, I…"

"You what?" He pressed in, using the weight of his body to add to the pressure on her windpipe. "What is it, Sandie? Are you sorry? For making me take time off work when we could use the money? How about for making me drive down here to get your ass and haul it back to Virginia? Are you sor—"

His voice slid into a scream as a well worn blade came down into his forearm, wedging itself deeply into Robert's thick flesh. He howled and released Sandra and she dropped to the floor, her knees cracking on impact. Even so, she managed to crawl under the dining room table for cover. While there, she was able to get a good look at the hatchet's owner.

"You. You go away," the man said, his coveralls dusty and crusted with dried dirt and grass. He hadn't come in the front door, Sandra thought madly. *Did he?* He was tall, taller than Robert even, with hunched shoulders as though he had tried to hide his size all his life. His hair was buzzed short, masking where his hairline had begun to recede, but the fuzz was a dark brown, making his sweaty scalp and prominent ears the focus. The rest of his face, thin lips and narrow, pointed nose—could pick a pea from a jug with that nose, Gramma used to say—was unremarkable save for the look of worry in his mismatched, yet earnest eyes as he wiggled the hatchet out of Robert's arm and raised it again.

"Fuck you, you ugly fuck." Robert said and pulled his service revolver from its holster. He aimed and squeezed off two rounds and the tall man jerked under the impact, releasing the weapon as he stumbled backward into the bar of the kitchen. The man grasped at the marble bar top to stop his fall, sending plates and cups crashing to the floor around him. Robert rushed up to the man where he slumped and kicked the body in the side with his boot.

Sandra cringed where she crouched under the table, knowing what impact those steel toed boots could have, as she watched her husband lean down to check to see if the threat had been dealt with appropriately.

Mom. She had to see if her mother was okay. Sandra had seen her fall, had heard the stomach-turning crack when she'd collided with the floor. She hadn't seen if the crack had been a hip, or her head. At forty, Sandra knew the toll a fall could take, knew the aches and pains a sound punching left on her body. Her mother couldn't take that at her age. The fall alone could have broken her bones.

No. It had been her choice to marry Robert. Her parents had been cautiously happy for her when she'd called to tell them, unsure at the reason for such a brief engagement period. But they were unsophisticated in the nuances associated with abusive relationships and did not know to counsel her.

In the back of her mind, she knew the signs had been there from the beginning: the way he'd dealt with the young barista for getting his coffee order wrong, bringing her to tears; the blatant disregard he had for the female officers; the way he spoke to his own mother. But her clock had been ticking, about to sound an alarm for end of baby-making time, and she'd heeded nature's call to procreate. But in two years of marriage, no children had come. When she'd suggested Robert get tested for fertility, as she already had been, the first hit came. Of course, he'd apologized by explaining that he'd lashed out because of his shock and hurt.

Stupidly, she'd carried on with him, adapting her behavior with each hit, each round of beatings, trying to predict what would light the fuse of his anger, only to have it change before her eyes. Weeks would go by with no hits, then she'd forget to run the dishwasher.

No sound came from the bathroom. Mamma, she thought, I'm sorry to bring this mess to you. I should have left years ago. I should have reported Robert the first time it happened. I just couldn't admit I chose the wrong man. There were so many choices she should have made. But there was still a chance to make this right.

Sandra crawled from under the table, her knees aching from where they pressed against the hardwood, and pushed herself carefully to her feet. She scanned the room for Robert's presence. He'd satisfied himself that the man was subdued and was in the kitchen wrapping one of her mother's good dishcloths around the wound in his arm. She walked, wobbly but determined, over to him. He watched her approach, gun holstered, confident he could handle her bare handed.

"Let's go," she said, surprised at the confidence in her voice.

Robert seemed taken aback as well, but that may have been the shock from his injury settling in. "Go where?"

"Let's go home."

He looked at her, suspicion clouding his squinty eyes. "What? You ready to go home now that your mutant in shining armor is down for the count?" He sneered before he nudged the man on the floor again with his foot. No response from the gangly body.

When she didn't respond to his taunt, he continued. "How do I know you ain't gonna pull this shit again, Sandie? Huh?" He reached out for her, then cursed again as the slice in his arm released another gout of blood.

"You leave my mother alone and you'll never have to worry about me ever again. I'll be the good wife you've always wanted. And then some. You let me check on my mom, and take her to the hospital if she needs it, then we will leave." Sandra reached in the drawer and threw a clean towel at him. "That and you swear to never lay eyes on her again."

"So you're bargaining with me now?"

Sandra looked the man she'd married almost four years ago, where he stood in her mother's beautiful new kitchen sweaty and bleeding, a look of hooded viciousness in his eyes. Like a dog that pretends to be friendly, then sinks his teeth into you once you're comfortable and reach out to pet him. But she could handle this mutt by not giving him his treats, not giving him the fear he craved. *Sacrifices, we all make them, sweet pea.* Her mother had said right before the wedding. *You just be sure to make the right ones.*

Her stomach churned and she felt lightheaded, swaying on her feet from the overload of adrenaline and lack of food. She steadied herself by grabbing onto the faucet and leaning her head against the cabinet above the sink. "Yes, I am. Do you accept?"

Robert watched her, his eyes taking in everything: her exhaustion, her resignation, and he seemed to accept her offer. In fact, he looked like a man who had managed to storm the castle's defenses, slay the dragon, and steal the princess. "Yeah. Yeah, I accept." His laugh came out as a snort and he wiped a viscous film of perspiration from his head with his undamaged sleeve. "I'm surprised that after all this you're trusting me to keep a promise."

From the corner of her eye, Sandra saw a flash of movement, possibly from the back bedroom or from the living room, it was hard to tell. She was so tired. Bone weary. Her head swam, but she was determined to do this. She could hold it together for a little while longer. Sandra stiffened when she felt Robert's hand on her arm, caressing the exposed skin there. His rough caress moved up to her face, then to her straggly ponytail, which was now loose and floppy from his earlier attentions.

"Maybe was can start again, Sandie. You know, wipe the slate blank. It'll be easier once we're back in Virginia. When we're home, There'll be no one to bother us, no one sticking their nose in our lives. Maybe I can start to trust you again." He ran his fingers down her neck and over down over her breasts. "Do you trust me, Sandie?" When his hands brushed over her throat, she winced. Robert pulled his hand away just as the butt of the hatchet crashed down on the back of his head.

"No," Sandra said. A crunch like the crack of a lobster shell sounded in the room. His body went slack as he crashed to the floor.

"I thought you were going to chop his head off." Sandra sagged against the bar top, and stared at her husband's body, unsure if he was alive or dead. She trembled as she realized it might be the latter.

"No," Mrs. Case said, lowering the hatchet carefully to the throw rug in the hall. "That much blood would have ruined my new floors. This is all hardwood, you know."

"He made such a mess." Blood was everywhere; pieces of glass and china figurines littered the floor. She looked around at her mother's new condo and the tears burned her eyes. Her mother slid over and hugged her tight. "I'm so sorry, Mom. Your beautiful place is a mess."

"Long as you're not ruined, my baby. That's what I care about." Her mother clucked over the mess as she picked up pieces of broken stoneware.

Sandra was aghast. "Mom, what do we do with—"

"I'll take care of it." Both women looked at the man towering over them with the pasty skin and disproportionate ears. Two holes were burned into the blue shoulder of his coveralls, but no other mark was on him.

"How—how is he alive?" Sandra looked back and forth between her mother and the man.

"Oh, he's been through much worse. Right, Jackie?" When the man nodded, Sandra's mother patted him on the shoulder. "Miss Maggie's grandson had a gang member after him and it got handled right away. That's why this place is so good."

The man was crouched over Robert, methodically lifting his arms and legs as if weighing them. "I can fix it." He wrung his large hands, his eyes darting between both women.

"You sure, Jackie, honey?"

"Yes, Ma'am. I can do it. Double quick."

"Okay," her mother said. "You be careful, now."

The hulking man began his work, separating Robert into manageable parts and removing all trace of him from the condo. Sandra found she couldn't turn away from the spectacle until her mother called her to help take the broken dishes out to the patio for recycling. When they returned, not a piece of Robert was left. Later the sound in the wall returned.

"It's one of Jackie's machines," her mother explained as she poured three cups of tea. "I think might have told you—it's a chipper or a grinder. Comforting, isn't it?"

Rhythm

Bay kou bliye, pòte mak sonje.

The giver of the blow forgets, the carrier of the scar remembers.

-Haitian proverb

With the slow beating of the tanbou, David drew Ezili Danto to his fire. He sensed the spirit mother lurking close, not yet ready to allow him to see her. Tangy salt air sagged under the weight of her presence. The scent of vetiver accompanied her, crisp with wild grasses and smoky with ash. His bare toes itched where they curled into the dry dirt of the Haitian mountainside. Drumbeats thudded against the darkening sky and echoed off the dilapidated buildings clinging to the cliffs. The promise of rain hung just out of reach.

He felt born to this land and its pulsing, eerie music. It swelled within him, growing, feeding.

No stage performance had given him the feeling of pride he felt from learning the intricate tempos native to the tanbou. He'd played the bongos in Cuba and the djembe in West Africa without the surge of power that surrounded him tonight. On the plane, he'd questioned the wisdom of coming here in the midst of the country's devastation and his own inner turmoil. The books and the movies didn't do it justice, but his grandfather's stories were right. Magic lived on this island, thriving like a rare species not seen anywhere else in the world.

David continued to play, enticing the ancient *lwa* with feral music from the taut drum. Friction from hours of practice had thickened the skin of his palms. The goatskin drumhead warmed under his touch and vibrated with sound.

He shifted on the hard soil. The drummer drew in a deep breath and released a jubilant cry to the heavens, celebrating the feeling like coming home.

***

In a small shop, David pointed to a drum where it sat on the dusty floor, wrapped with rough rope. Reaching almost to his waist, the instrument looked as though hands had shaped it on a potter's wheel: large round body atop a tapered base. Strips of bright cloth, a scattering of blue and yellow and green, coiled around its entire length. "How about this one?"

"Ah, good choice. For a memory of your time here," the shop owner said, his wrinkled hands patting it to send a hollow echo through the tiny store. "Hand made of softwood from the—"

"Petwo nation. I know." At the shop owner's raised eyebrow, he explained. "My grandfather came here in the thirties when the Marines occupied Haiti. What he didn't tell me, I learned on my own. Mwen pale kreyòl."

The man laughed at David's pronunciation. "Good try. You a scholar? That why you come to Port au Prince?"

"I'm here to learn, but I'm no scholar."

He peered at David with sun-weary eyes. "I know you. I see you before. You come with other blans to rebuild schools and clean wells."

"Did you just call me white?" He lifted a coiled dreadlock to call the man's attention to his coarse, thick hair. David was from the Carolinas, where any duskiness of skin tone automatically put you in the category of black—or to a larger extent, the category of "You must got some kinda black in you, son. Or maybe Indian."

118

There was camaraderie in that—a certain safety—knowing your darker skin gave you a sense of community with others of color. He hadn't realized the pleasure he took in the slight nod of recognition blacks gave each other back home, even if they didn't know you. The loss of that acknowledgement left another hole in him—this one smaller, but deep and weeping.

"You not from Haiti, so you blan no matter what color you is." He lifted his shoulders in an elaborate shrug, hands out, pale ivory palms contrasting with espresso-tinted skin.

"How much?" David asked.

"For you, a deal. Half price. In thanks for helping my country." He quoted a nominal figure.

Half price was still a substantial profit for the man. "I'll pay full price if it comes with lessons."

The Haitian's eyes went wide. "You want to play tanbou? Why? To get a woman in your bed?"

"I want to call a spirit."

The man turned and spat on the floor. "You playing, right? You play with Vodou? I do not help you make such jokes."

"No, nothing like that. I respect the ways of Vodou. That's why I'm here. One of the reasons, anyway. I want to call on a spirit goddess for guidance."

"Which one?"

"I have the money. Will you teach me?"

Indecipherable Haitian Creole accompanied the shop owner's noncommittal shrug as the man turned to go back to his counter.

"Fine. I want to call Danto."

"What you know about Ezili Danto?" The man glanced around as though the ancestral misté could hear him.

"I need advice to deal with a problem."

"Your problem not money. Love, maybe? You need her sister Ezili Freda. She gentle and will help your heart."

"No, it has to be Danto."

"Ah, I see. You want someone to suffer." He snorted laughter and stuck a toothpick from his shirt pocket between his teeth. "You a fool. She will not come to you. You not Haitian."

"A fool willing to pay for your time, so it's no loss to you."

The shopkeeper considered the offer. "I don't sit the circle with you."

"Then I'll sit alone."

"Yes. That is good."

Alone in a clearing with the colorful drum between his thighs, David pounded out a beat to bring the spirit to his fire. His arms ached and his back throbbed. When he shifted position because his legs had fallen asleep, they stung like they were pierced with fire-tipped needles.

She came closer, dancing with the writhing flames as they lapped at her midnight skin. Moonlight kissed oiled flesh. Impossibly long arms flapped like sailcloth in an ocean breeze. Powerful thigh muscles bunched when she leapt into the air. The spirit's chosen form leaked sweat as she danced to the primal call of the tanbou. Ezili's face, painted chalk-white, bore no expression, but a red, angry scar blazed on her right cheek.

He continued to play.

Her full breasts were bare to the night and they swayed to the tempo of his hands. David was unable to look away from her hips as they jerked back and forth as if in orgasm, giving glimpses of round buttocks swathed in the short dried grass skirt. He felt himself grow hard, his erection pressing against the side of the drum.

Ezili Danto circled the fire like a jungle beast: unafraid of man, secure in her superiority. He had been able to bring her this close, to see the lone drummer dressed in the white robe of an oungan.

The ground beneath David pulsed with heat and sweat crawled down his back. He called out to the spirit, praising her as the shopkeeper had instructed. "Come to my fire, Danto, whose eyes bring the storms. Feel the music of my hands and counsel me."

David thumped the hides, alternating palms, thumbs, and fingers. The scent of sweet sap and resin teased his nose as the nimble creature swayed to the primal beats. His palms thudded against the drumhead and his vision wavered in the heat and smoke. She seemed an illusion, her form a quivering mirage in this devastated tropic.

He rocked back and forth without realizing it, caught between his world and hers. Ezili's broad feet stomped, creating a blurred whirlwind of dust and gravel, as her dancing outpaced the drummer.

David sped up, desperate to keep pace. His little finger caught the edge of the rope holding the drum together. He heard a crack and cried out in pain, clutching his injured digit.

The fire blazed up with a sharp hiss, then vanished as if blown out, leaving him in darkness.

***

Morning rose, hot and oppressive as David entered the shop, already drenched in sweat and frustration.

"So. Your circle was good?"

David cursed as the shopkeeper gripped his hand. "Not exactly."

"You alive. You here. Is good." Amusement danced around the man's eyes and he scratched at his coarse salt and pepper beard.

"I couldn't keep up long enough. She disappeared when I stopped playing."

The rheumy eyes sharpened and David felt their gaze jab at him like a stick. "Stop? Why you stop? If you want her, nothing can make you stop."

"The ropes came loose and I caught my finger. I think I broke it on that piece of shit drum."

The man sucked at his teeth in disgust. "That why you stop? A finger? You are not enough for her."

"You don't understand. My hands are my life. They're how I earn my living."

"I understand you not ready for Danto."

"No, I am. I'm ready." His voice hardened as he squared his shoulders. "I only have a few more days. I can do this."

"It take a lifetime to master tanbou and make it speak like the voice of mistés. Without that, there is no Vodou."

"I've been drumming since I was eight years old, man. I got her attention once and I can do it again. And this time, nothing will get me to stop. "

A gust of sea air blew open the frail shop door like an angry customer. David shivered in the cool breeze and pulled the shirt away from his damp back with quick, sharp jerks.

"You ask no small thing." The Haitian ambled over to the door and glanced outside before closing it. He leaned against the doorframe as he continued. "Make for her a path. Maybe she use it, maybe she don't. But there is danger, drummer."

"I'll be careful."

"Think that matter?"

David didn't reply. "Has anyone you know ever seen her?"

"Oh, yes. But none see the same Danto."

"What's that mean?"

"Some say she like a mother protecting her child. Some say she come like a new lover, sweet and hot." He pulled the drum to him. "Some say nothing."

"Nothing? Why?"

"Some do not speak of the time with her. Or they cannot."

"What's your take on all of this? What do you say?"

"I say she come in the way you need." His smile took the sting out of his next words. "But she will not come to you no way, so?"

He pocketed David's money and sat on an overturned barrel. "Listen." He looked into the younger man's eyes as he gave his final lesson, a heated duple meter beat. His dark, gnarled hands were stark against the ivory colored drumhead. "No food, you play. No rest, you play." His eyes closed and his head tilted, as if he were listening to someone whispering a secret in his ear. "No pain can make you stop. She takes your everything."

David's gaze slid away from the older man's and he ran a finger over a callous on the base of his thumb. "My everything is already gone."

He told Connie he wanted to help with the relief efforts. "Do you want to come with me? We could do a lot."

"To Haiti? Are you crazy?" Her neat, trim brows crinkled in a frown and she bit her lip.

"Connie, you're an RN, you could help more than I can. We don't have to stay long. A week, ten days. If it's okay with you, I might stay a little longer, but I think it'd be an amazing experience."

She twisted the ring on her left hand. "I don't think so. But you go. It would be great publicity for a member of the band to be seen over there."

David took her face in his hands. "I know you hate it when I go on tour and you think this is just another trip to keep us apart. But I promise when I get back, we'll go somewhere together." He kissed her and hugged her close. "Once we make the big time, it'll all be worth it."

Connie pulled away first. "I know. I'll be fine. There's plenty for me to do here."

"That's 'cause you're my girl. Don't forget I'm getting my vaccinations after work today. Did you know I have to get close to ten shots for this visit?"

She smiled. "Better you than me."

Under a clear, star filled sky, David built the fire twice as large this time, the memory of betrayal sharp and acidic in his mind. He bound his fingers with tape like a boxer before a match and began to play. Gentle winds shushed the slums into silence. Rickety doors remained shut tight against the ancestral spirits.

No one stirred.

Both of David's hands caressed the tanbou and the sound rolled off the taut goatskin in aching waves. The beats lengthened, grew deeper, into a slow and loping gait. As the music rose, it gained confidence and strode forward with sure steps.

Faster now, short smacks of open palm mixed with thumps of closed fist. Divergent, each hand marked a necessary dissonance to appease the quick, demanding spirit. He created an image of Connie's face in his mind, lips parted in ecstasy, and used it like a lens to focus his pain and draw the vengeful Danto's attention.

His left thumb struck the drumhead in the center. The thumb clung and slid over the goatskin, leaving a weary moan on the night air. He squeezed his eyes shut against the hot tears pricking his lids. The wail of the drum joined his heart's cry for justice.

When he opened his eyes again, Ezili sat across the fire from him. Still as stone, she waited, her red eyes reflecting the dancing flames. The scar on her cheek bled freely now. Tendrils of fear coiled around his heart. A female voice ground its way into his head. *Tell me your story.*

He did.

> *Connie's iPod was in the speaker when he got home, its volume turned close to maximum. The player blared electrified noise into his skull and a headache had started by the time he reached the kitchen.*
>
> *"Hey, babe," he yelled. "The doc changed my appointment to tomorrow. They got really busy this afternoon." He realized the uselessness of yelling over the music and went to look for his fiancée.*
>
> *He found her in the den. She lay back on the leather couch, legs wide, with her mouth open. Her long hair curled along the arm of the sofa as she*

bucked under the enthusiastic pumping of a burly, tattooed man.

The sight of her, splayed open, welcoming the brute into her was more than he could stand. His head pounded, too tight for his brain. Breath came in great gulping heaves as fury burned a hole in his chest big enough for his heart to fall through.

No, not again.

David started toward the couple. So engrossed in pleasure, neither of them noticed him. A veil of anger dropped over his eyes and the room went red. He looked around for something sharp. For something heavy.

Not this time…

He backed out of the room, unable to yank his gaze from their entwined bodies, until the door closed behind him, Connie's moans the soundtrack for his plans.

Ezili's shadowy form slipped through the half-light of the fire as she roiled to the drum's cacophony. Chalky paint made her face look as rough as coconut skin. She swiveled her elongated head toward him.

David's shoulders began to slump, but he jerked himself upright. His back protested the hours he'd sat on the unforgiving ground with loud, painful pops and his eyes burned with fatigue and grit. The spirit slunk closer, drawn by the tortured music. Her essence surrounded him, pressed in on his body and his soul.

Balmy wind amplified the whispered words, bringing her promise to him again and again with each passing breeze. On hands and knees, she crept closer until all David could see were her eyes.

In those almond-shaped orbs, red and white swirled together. His breath slowed as he stared into their depths.

Under her marbled gaze, his heartbeat shifted and changed to mimic the one coming from his hands. Ezili ran her hands down his shoulders and over his chest in a caress, the tips of her fingers disappearing inside his skin. She trailed her fingers over his lap and his penis responded, straining like a divining rod. Although her face didn't change, he could feel her pleased laughter in his mind.

She is stupid girl.

David shuddered as she enfolded him in her long arms, surrounding him with fierce protection. Through the steamy air, coldness pierced him like a blade as the ancient spirit's will displaced his own. All that was David moved aside, cowering in her presence.

"Not like this. I don't want—"

The young man trembled in shock and fear while Ezili pressed in, smothering him like an overbearing mother. She filled him like boiling oil, searing his soul with flashing quickness. It left his body shuddering as his hands spasmed on the drumhead, playing an unintentional beat, sharp with the tang of acidic sweat. He was full, near to bursting, and he panted with the effort of speech. "What...are you going...to do?"

Silans, she soothed. *I fix for you.*

"But how?"

Set koud kouto, set koud pwenyad. Even with his limited knowledge of the language, her words and intent were clear.

Seven stabs of the knife, seven stabs of the sword.

***

Two days later, David sauntered into the tiny shop and browsed the plentiful knick-knacks and wooden carvings while the owner sold bottles of mango soda to a group of sweating relief workers. He picked up a wide-eyed doll, its face round and shiny black, and ran his fingers over the rough cotton dress and headscarf. He snorted as he read the tag attached to it.

"Ah, you have returned, drummer."

"I wanted to say good-bye. I leave today."

"Your problem is no more?"

"I'll take care of it as soon as I get back. Thank you for your help."

"It is nothing."

David's pupil and iris swirled together with the white of his eye. He turned the doll over, his calloused fingers snagging the cloth as he switched to fluid Haitian. "Jean-Pierre. Is this what my people think I look like?"

"Those that have not seen you as you truly are." The old man shrugged his narrow shoulders. "It is what they are comfortable with because it makes them feel less afraid."

"Even so, it is good to be without this for a while." David stroked his right cheek, unmarked under a light growth of stubble.

"You are always beautiful to me," Jean-Pierre said.

"Thank you for this one. Much time has passed since a blan has come to me." David loosened the rope around the tanbou and unwound bands of blue and yellow cloth. "He says he does not wish her death, but in time, he will see my way." A wedge of wood from the drum's side had been removed and whittled sharp, its point already dark with blood. It fit flush into the shallow cavity, undetectable when he re-wrapped the drum.

128

"Forever, I am your servant, Danto."

"This will be such a joy." David smiled. "I will return soon, you know I cannot stay away for long."

He left the old Haitian standing in the doorway, staring after him as he walked the dusty path to the airport, drum slung over his shoulder, his fingers tapping a divine rhythm.

The Choking Kind

An old man sat behind the dilapidated counter of the country store humming Negro spirituals as Grace walked in, sweaty from standing in the Charleston sun. Her new black dress clung to her like a frightened child and she plucked at its neckline with irritation.

"Sun hot for all that there, *enny?*" He put down his newspaper, folded to the obituary page and nodded at her ensemble. She smiled at his words, the singsong of her native Gullah reaching her ears for the first time in almost a decade. English peppered with African dialects made a steamy fusion of language rich with chewy rhythms.

"Too hot to be wearing black, that's for sure." Funny how her drawl had returned, each vowel emerging pregnant, full and round. "But I just came from a funeral," Grace said. She shook her head, surprised at her revelation. Half a day here and she was already over sharing with strangers.

She wove her way through the tight aisles of the old store. Dusty tin cans lined the shelves, some bearing labels promoting brand names long out of production.

Grace pulled her braids away from where they lay heavy against her damp neck. In the few hours she'd been at the cemetery, the sun had turned her skin the color of burnished teak. Sticky heat formed a staunch wall around the island, blocking all but the most steadfast of breezes. What wind managed to penetrate was off the salt marsh and dank with sulfur, smelling like a match just blown out. Afternoon slipped toward dusk and the island's night creatures would soon come alive.

But her father wouldn't. No amount of prayer or hoodoo could do that. She wiped perspiration from her face.

The storeowner took in her designer handbag and shades. Then his gaze traveled to the window, smoky with age and inattention, where her car waited outside in the dried grass. He asked with a healthy serving of doubt, "You a *binyuh*?"

"Yessir. Grew up in the last house on Marsh Road." She looked at the date on the bottom of a can and put it back on the shelf. "Though the last time I was here, that road didn't even have a name."

A smile warmed the old man's face, softening the deep ebony lines. "Then you been gone a long time."

Wadmalaw Island had escaped time's notice; its residents caught fish and shrimp exactly as they had when they'd been brought to this land as slaves. Shopping consisted of makeshift roadside stands manned by heat-softened proprietors of intricate sweetgrass baskets and hand-harvested produce.

"Pretty gal like you aine wed?"

She smiled, lips tight. "Nope." There'd been enough discussion of marriage lately and she needed a break from her latest beau's persistence. Grace placed her items on the counter for purchase: quarter bushel of peaches, Mason jar of clear moonshine, spearmint gum.

"You said you was here for services. Who you lost?"

"My Pop. Joseph Moultrie. Did you know him?"

He gathered her purchases in a line before he meticulously pressed buttons on an ancient wooden cash register. "Once, way back. Kept to hisself the last few years, though."

Grace pursed her lips. "I'm not surprised. We had a bit of a falling out over a… family issue. I left but he was happy staying right in that little house at the top of the road."

The man nodded in understanding, of which part of her comment she didn't know. "Never guessed you was his. Rugged old so-and-so." He lifted his arm, palm toward the ceiling. "Bless the dead."

"Yeah, he was. Guess I must look like my Ma, then. But I don't remember her."

"Neither me," he said. The man's lip trembled as he focused his attention on packing her purchases.

"You knew my father that long ago, but not my mother? See, that's why I left this place." She twisted a cowrie shell fastened to the end of a plait. "Nobody wants to talk about her. I can almost understand Pop not wanting to talk about her, but I can't get a word out of anyone. They're both dead now. Who cares?"

"Joe never crack teeth 'bout your Ma and I won't neither."

"Thought you said you didn't know her."

"Don't."

"Would you help me with something?"

He quoted her a price, but kept his eyes on the buttons of the register as he grunted in inquiry. "Hmm?"

"Directions. To Ma's grave."

When he didn't respond, she realized he was waiting for her payment. "Oh, sorry." Grace placed cash in his cupped palm and dropped the coins he gave her as change into a cracked ashtray on the counter. He busied himself with finding the right sized bag for her purchases.

Grace raised her voice, thinking the man hadn't heard her earlier question. "I've been to Pop's grave. Now I need to visit my Ma's."

His fingers shook, either with nerves or age. After several tries, he was able to separate one brown paper bag from the stack.

Grace plucked the Mason jar of moonshine from the bag and put it in her purse. Its weight, along with that of a worn Bible she'd found hidden in a beat-up hatbox in Pop's closet, made her purse strap bite into her shoulder. "Do you know where she's buried? Pop never told me anything."

He seemed to deflate, becoming smaller, flatter. "She aine..." He ran a crumpled handkerchief over his damp forehead. "I don't believe she dead."

Grace stared at him, speechless until he patted the worn metal stool next to the counter and she perched on it. The old man found two dented tin cups under the counter and he pointed at her purse where she'd put the bottle of shine. She relinquished the jar to him and he poured a generous amount for each of them.

"He told me that she died." But Pop had never allowed trips to the cemetery or even conversation about her mother. At first, he distracted her with toys or candies. As she got older, he simply ignored her pleas for information, telling her to do her schoolwork. "For years he told me that."

He drained his cup and filled another before he spoke. "She somewhere deep in that marsh. But dead? I aine sure."

Despite the struggles of the window unit air conditioner, it was stifling in the store. Grace waved a cardboard fan she'd gotten at her father's services in front of her face. "I've got to get in that grave," she said. "I have to know if she's dead."

He avoided her intense gaze as he sliced up a ripe peach from her bag and mashed its pulpy sweet flesh into the next cup of moonshine. "No way you getting in that place unless you a witch. And you don't look no where close to being no boo-hag." He took another long swig, draining the cup. A moment later, he pulled the gnawed peach skin out of his mouth and placed it delicately in the graying handkerchief.

Boo-hag. She'd been no more than seven or eight when Pop's mama had come to visit and told her stories of the swamp witches. They existed on male lust, sucking it in like air, leaving their willing hosts drained and temporarily paralyzed. Unwilling ones were left dead. Pop had come in during the middle of the tale and forbidden any more nonsense talk.

"I remember those stories."

"Just stories, huh?"

"I don't know," Grace shifted her purse higher on her arm. "Pop used to throw salt over his shoulder when he spilled it. A couple of people at the funeral told me they'd already seen his spirit walking on the roadside." She frowned. "I don't feel... alone sometimes. So I stopped saying things don't exist a long time ago."

The old man nodded.

"I need to get into that grave, though," she said.

"No way you can pass through clean 'cept..." He stopped, cursed his loose tongue. "Damn backyard shine. Gets to me quick."

Grace sat up, rocking the stool forward. "Except what?"

He lifted the cup to his lips, then changed his mind and sat it down again. "The one way I know aine worth it."

"Please tell me."

"What you know 'bout hags?"

"Not much. They steal a man's..." She groped for a word. "Desire and make him weak."

"More than that sometime, but that's what the old people say," he said, seemingly oblivious to his own age. "But how?"

Grace stuck a piece of gum into her mouth and shrugged. "Magic, I guess. I don't know."

"Without they skin, that's how." He leaned back in the ancient chair. "Don't screw up your face like that. You asked for the tale, now you aine ready for it?"

"Okay, sorry. Tell me."

"Get one of them hags to help you. They all over them woods after midnight." He poured the rest of the shine into his cup. "You can't get in that graveyard smelling like you fresh out the womb. They say that thing old Joe got guarding the place'll rip you apart."

***

Grace crouched behind a thick-rooted oak tree in the densest part of the woods. Spanish moss hung from the trees filtering the moonlight like lace curtains as she watched the group of witches congregate around small piles of what looked to be heaps of discarded laundry. She moved closer inches at a time, praying that her progress through the forest sounded like an animal skittering for safety.

Even though the old man had said to steal one, Grace couldn't bring herself to do it. So she'd waited in moonlit darkness for hours, going through flashlight batteries and sticks of gum, until the hags returned from their carousing. Her only hope was that they would appreciate her manners for asking politely.

As she got nearer, Grace could see that the heaps of laundry were actually piles of luminous sky blue flesh lying in puddles on the ground. The creatures standing above them were grotesque, wet and blood red, as they stood in line to run their fingers over each pile, stage whispering. Grace strained to hear the grainy, singsong words of the figure in front as they floated toward her on puffs of dogwood-scented wind.

Skin, skin, skinny... Do you know me?

Skin, skin, skinny... Is you mine?

The first pile didn't move, so the stooped creature repeated itself to the second. No response. But the words made the third heap quiver and spring from the damp ground and dangle suspended in air as if on a hanger. Grace stared openmouthed as the witch donned the grisly garment and flew off, out of the woods. Other hags followed a similar ritual as the piles of flesh dwindled. Soon only one hag remained.

"I know you are there, child. Come to me." The boo-hag didn't turn to face her, but Grace heard its voice, soft and persuasive, clearly over the pounding of her own heart.

Grace swallowed, throat dry as her hands clutched the rough bark of the ancient tree. The witch didn't give any other indication that she'd spoken as she stepped into her suit of flesh. It covered her slimy-looking frame without leaving any indication of an opening.

"I know you've been watching me with those marble eyes of yours. Curiosity shines in the dark." She stood with her back to Grace, as she basked naked in the rays of moonlight. "Are you embarrassed?"

The hag slipped on a faded cotton dress from the forest floor. It was difficult to tell the color—it may have been green or brown or black—as it melded with the night so well. She made no attempt to tame her rioting hair. "There now. Come see what you wish to see."

Grace's tongue loosened. "I don't want..." Her whisper trailed off as she realized lying to a witch woman was not a good idea.

"Oh, but you do." The boo-hag turned to Grace with the speed of a striking snake.

The young woman shrieked and shuffled backward, landing on her bottom in a scattering of decaying leaves. Backlit by the gibbous moon, the hag peeled herself away from her surroundings. Her eyes looked empty at first, but as she came closer, Grace saw they were solid and shiny black, like patent leather.

To Grace's surprise, the crone laughed. "Which is it? Frightening? Disgusting? Better with the skin?"

Gone was the gory, dripping muscle-over-bone. Over it lay a washing powder blue husk that hung loose on the hag's slight physique. The witch's voice belied her look, because the demand came out silky and lulling. "Speak your mind."

There was no need to be coy. Any person of sound mind would be home in bed, not stalking boo-hags for favors in the middle of the night. She scrambled to her feet. "I need to get into my Ma's grave."

"LuAnn Moultrie's grave? What for?"

"How do you know my mother?"

"I've been roaming these woods since before you were thought of. I see a lot and hear a lot more." Frowning made the witch look as though her face were going to separate down the middle. "Doesn't matter though. You can't get out there because your Pa set a spell on that land."

"I know. But someone told me I might be able to get by the guard dog if you…" She trailed off, the right words eluding her.

"If you were to look and smell like a hag? That why you're so taken with my skin?"

"Yes, Ma'am."

The hag laughed, a controlled shriek. "Been a long time since anyone called me that. You might be able to do it if you could fool that plat-eye." She turned serious again. "A plat-eye is no a dog. Ever seen one?"

Grace shook her head.

"He'll get close to smell you, check you out. Don't run and you'll be fine. Run and it's the end of you, skin or no."

"I understand."

"Um hm." Heat rushed into Grace's face as the witch's gaze journeyed over her. "What do you have to offer?"

"Offer?" Grace's jaw went slack. "I don't have anything. I thought—"

"You thought me that generous?" The creature extended a hand ending in gnarled, overgrown claws. "Or were you proposing an exchange?"

This time Grace held her ground. "No!"

"Good girl," the hag said, approval evident in her tone. "Now what do you have that I might want?"

"Money?"

Another shriek. "Try again."

"My car?"

"We fly, girl. On the wind or without it." Her smile returned. "You could owe me."

Grace rubbed her arms for warmth even in the balmy night air. Part of her wanted to run away and check into a hotel. To leave at first light and forget that she ever lived on this island. Reinvent herself again. "Okay," she whispered. "But what is a plat-eye?"

"Pieces of dead animals put together and brought back to life." The hag reached up to her mane of coarse graying hair. As Grace watched, it appeared she was going to smooth it with her palms.

Instead, she parted the mass of steel wool hair and pulled. With a sucking pop, the hide separated and the hag shrugged it off like a winter coat. The skin swung in the air like a hanged man. "You don't know nothing about what you getting mixed up in and well, I'm sorry for you."

Rogue thoughts dashed through her mind, chased by the thought of Pop's scrawled words in the old Bible she found tucked in an old shoebox.

I was a good man before you.

Grace reached for the skin and it came toward her, lowering itself several inches to her height. Even with the eye sockets empty, the hide seemed to be looking at her, assessing her worthiness to wear it. Where she touched it, the skin felt cool like crisp bed linen. Her stomach roiled and she suppressed a shudder before she stepped into the opening down the back, clothes and all.

Inside the skin was hot, sticky with blood and ripe with the scent of bowel. Grace gagged at the moist, dank stench. "You can do this, Grace," she muttered. She held her breath as she pulled it over her face and it sealed itself closed. With a bit of adjusting she was able to breathe from the mouth and nose and see out of the eyeholes, but the world had a strange look, as though it were covered in plastic wrap. For a moment, the skin hung loose as it had on the witch, then it fused itself to her body with a rubbery snap. "Oh God," she gasped, the shells on her braids pressing into the tender skin of her neck.

The hag didn't comment on her blasphemous outcry. Instead, she leapt into the air, calling over her shoulder. "Be back by sunup or I'm coming for my hide."

"How do I get there?"

"Skinny knows the way." Before she could respond, the hag flew away, leaving Grace alone as the shuffling sounds of the night returned to the woods.

Walking was no easy task in the weighty husk. Each movement was the result of deliberate thought and twice the usual amount of effort. Grace was panting by the time she crossed the woods and reached the borders of the overgrown plot of land where her father had supposedly laid her mother to rest. She'd been so focused on moving that Grace was almost on top of the guard beast before she saw it.

The creature's wide back reached Grace's waist and it was covered in various types of fur: long and black and shaggy in some places, smooth and golden and close to its barrel-shaped body in others. She stood stock still as it approached. The plat-eye's pig snout twitched as it sniffed at her offered hand. Then it prodded her with its yellowing tusks. When it bumped its head under her hand, she realized what it wanted. Grace petted the dog-pig thing, ruffling its dusty, mismatched fur. The plat-eye snorted, sat back on its four hind legs and purred.

"I can pet you more later, but I need to find the grave you're guarding." She saw a mound covered in creeping ivy a few paces away. "Is that it?"

Grace knelt at the bottom of the mound and began to dig. She'd brought the small spade, but the hag skin didn't need it. It sensed she was trying to break through packed dirt and black earth. It rippled, fusing her thumb to the rest of her fingers to form her hands into makeshift shovels.

The plat-eye sat on its rear hind legs and scratched itself with one of its fore-hinds before coming over to investigate. It helped her dig; scratching the black dirt with paws the size of her palm. Movement was no easier as she grunted with the exertion of bending the bulky hide to her will. She was hot, sweating, trapped inside the skin with her own fear and her father's words.

So I used it, LuAnn. That little bit of magic you taught me. Pieces of animals I found. Only one I had to kill myself. When it rose up from the ground, I ain't shame to say I almost wet myself. Never seen nothing like that thing. Almost turned on me before I could finish the hex. But I did it. It's roaming round that tombstone. Nobody can get near, 'cept maybe you.

But you gone, ain't you, LuAnn? Left me with this child. I can raise her. Done a damn good job so far. But the girl is smart, starting to ask questions about her Ma.

Grace dug faster. Inhaling the turned dirt made her cough. Not enough time. Her digging became frantic as the words that fell from the Bible pages flew at her with each scoop of earth.

Had to make the headstone myself. Couldn't tell no one. Killing my wife. What righteous man does that?

She hit a hard spot. Grace slowed, used her spade-like hands to find the edges of the wooden box as the plat-eye whined. She soothed it. "Shh. It's okay, boy. We have to know, right?"

The dog-pig snorted, its tusks dark from rooting in the moist dirt. It crouched close by, red eyes solemn and watchful.

She wedged one of her shovel shaped hands under the lid of the handmade coffin. Grace had to stand up to get enough leverage to wedge it loose. For a moment she paused, questioning her own logic. Maybe it was better not to know.

What has been seen cannot be unseen. Grace couldn't remember where she'd heard those words, but at this moment, she believed that nothing could be truer. She'd come this far, making deals with blue-skinned crones, digging up her mother's grave by crescent moonlight.

Suppose Ma was in here and Pop had killed her. She ran the scoop of her hand along the loosened lid imagining a filthy, worm-eaten dress still showing slashes from a knife. Flaky blood dried to a spice color. She kept up a whispered litany: *I want to know. I want to know.* The hag's hide shimmered again and her fingers and thumb separated into hands.

Before she could change her mind, she threw off the coffin's lid.

Grace stood over the open box, eyes shut tight. She didn't open them until she felt the dog-thing winding around her legs, its fur bristly and its heavy tail thumping her leg, pushing her forward and off-balance.

Her eyes flew open. She put out her hands and landed on her knees, braced against the rough edges of the box. Splinters broke off the coffin and stuck in the blue. Grace didn't have the dexterity with her borrowed fingers to pull them out, so she left them where they were and looked inside.

There was no body.

A dress lay settled into a deep layer of brown dust: delicate white eyelet, now turned dry and tea-colored. Its long sleeves crossed over each other as though the wearer had been laid out lovingly and with reverence. Where the hands should have been, moonlight glinted off a small gold band. Grace plucked it from the box, the touch of her hand causing the papery dress to crumble into powder.

***

Close to sunup, Grace waited in the fleeing dark for the hag. She wasn't any wiser than she'd been when the night started. Her muscles hurt. Itchy with sweat, she was boiling inside the borrowed skin. All attempts to relieve her itch were blocked by the hag's thick hide. It was like trying to scratch herself through a blanket.

Mossy oak branches above her head rustled and the witch glided down to stand across from her. The scent of wood smoke surrounded her and the reflective eyes were sharp, assessing her skin and its wearer.

"Find what you looking for?"

"No." She was too tired to elaborate or notice the hag had drifted closer.

The hag whistled a short tune and the skin sprang to attention, dragging Grace up in the air, shaking her as it struggled to dislodge her body. She fell to the ground with a grunt.

After she made a sympathetic noise in Grace's direction, the hag asked for her payment. Grace looked at the bloody body standing next to its blue skin as they both gazed down at her. She pressed her back against the bark of the oak, exhausted and ready for this search to end. "I don't have anything. There was a coffin but the dress inside crumbled when I touched it."

Her sight hadn't adjusted after being inside the skin for so long. Everything still had a tight, shiny look to it and it was giving her a headache. Grace closed her eyes. Funny how the pain only started after the skin left her.

"All I found was this." She held the ring aloft.

With surprising gentleness, the witch accepted her payment. She was quiet so long that Grace opened her eyes. The world was lighter. Morning would break soon, but Grace was the only one aware of it.

"Your Pop was the kind of man all the girls wanted. Good-looking and didn't know it. But he saw me one night when I was wearing a new skin. Told me right then he was determined to marry me." The hag laughed without mirth, her voice thick with emotion. "Like a fool, I let him."

Grace sat dumbfounded, covered in foul-smelling gore, dried leaves and grit. And listened.

"Even wore this ring for a while. He had a root lady put a love spell on it, but I didn't mind him trying to trap me." She twisted the band of metal in her bent claws. "I already loved him. But soon, it was too much. Too tight. I got tired of that skin. Never taking it off. Never changing."

"What did you do?" It was her own story spoken to her through wide blue lips and she knew the answer. Run. Just as she'd done before this trip home.

"I wanted to tear it loose. Fling that skin far as I could. But one full moon Sunday night, you came, all sweet and fresh and new. And the feeling went away for a while. Then it returned, stronger." The hag took a deep trembling breath. "I had to go."

"Pop must have hated you."

"He knew one day I'd leave. Knew I'd try to come back, too. So he made me shed the face he loved, my whole skin." Her laugh was bitter. "Without me inside, it couldn't last. A few days, maybe. Then it dries up into nothing."

Grace pressed her fingertips to her temples to stop the heated throb behind her eyes. "I don't understand."

"It was so I couldn't be 'her' for anyone else." She knelt in front of Grace. "He buried that skin like he was having a funeral for me. Then he painted the house blue—my blue—knowing I couldn't enter after he did it, so I could never come back for you."

145

"He wouldn't," Grace pulled crumpled oak leaves from her pants. "He used to say he wished LuAnn could be here."

"He didn't consider me to be LuAnn any more. That was what he called me up until I was leaving." She stood. "Won't tell you what he called me then."

Grace remembered the falling pages. Shaky confessions written in knife-sharpened pencil. "He knew you were a... a...."

"Yes, and he thought he could fix me. Stop my roaming. But no." No-longer-LuAnn lifted her moist, patent leather eyes and Grace saw the muscles in her jaw and neck tighten. "Now do you understand why you can't stay with no man? His love gets too tight for you and you have to get loose or choke to death."

Grace leaned her head back against the tree, the shells on her braids a wind chime in the night. Memories of men she'd cared for danced to the unbidden tune. She was happy until they wanted to know where she was and what she was doing. They wanted to be able to tell her no and it was then she had to leave. Now her memories no longer included any of the men's names or faces. "But I want someone to love me," she whispered, ashamed of the admission.

"Never said you couldn't have love. Just not the choking kind." The witch blinked as the darkness of night lifted. "A time comes for all of us to change. No one is the same always." Quickly, she stepped into her skin, the one that changed—shed each person she no longer needed to be.

"Are you leaving?" Grace asked. She was full of more questions now than she'd been before she'd come.

"I have to go. For now." Grace thought she heard a hint of hesitation in her mother's smooth voice. "But I'll be here... around."

"Do something for me?" Grace asked.

146

"Not screaming to be rid of me yet?"

"You're my Ma," she said. The exertions of the night had caught up with her and she yawned. "Free the dog-thing. Nothing should be forced to stay in one place."

"Think you already did, my girl."

Grace turned and watched the plat-eye chase the last of the fireflies through the woods, leaping and pawing at them until he faded into the morning. When she turned back, her mother was gone.

***

It was time to leave.

But with her father buried on the banks of the marsh and her mother roaming the night, there was something to come back to. Maybe she could even talk Ma into teaching her a few spells. As she locked up the last house on Marsh Road, she decided to make a stop before leaving the island.

Grace pulled up to the corner store to say good-bye to the old man. The store was closed, dim inside. She peered through a grimy window and saw a figure standing over him where he lay crumpled in his chair like an expired coupon. Long and gangly with its meaty organs pulsing, the hag moved closer, its body glistening. She watched as it reached toward the man behind his counter.

A thought of helping him crossed her mind. Although she was no match for a true boo-hag, there had to be a way to save him.

From what? Maybe he wanted the witch here to drink the last of his life before he got too feeble. Too weak to run the store or give advice or gossip. She should leave him to enjoy his fate.

The hag's claws were on him now. A time comes for all of us...

As she turned away, Grace saw the husk of the old man rise up to dangle in the air and she heard the creature speak, its voice soft and lulling.

Skin, skin, skinny... Do you know me?

Acknowledgements

My sincerest appreciation goes out to my husband, whose patience is legendary. Thanks for putting up with all of my ideas that start with, "You know what I just thought of?" I love you.

Thank you to Mark Taylor for creating the cover for *Spook Lights* and formatting the text. You do excellent work—both in front and behind the writing scene.

To the authors who read versions of *Spook Lights* before the final: B.D. Bruns, Crystal Connor, and Roma Gray. I love your work. Thank you for reading mine.

To the Indigo Dreamers for reading some of these stories and giving feedback, for keeping me motivated to write, for empathizing, and for being the amazing, creative women you are. Thanks so much.

And to Jim Becker, who gave constructive feedback laced with just the right amount of snark. As you asked, I'm not mentioning you.

Publication History

"Doc Buzzard's Coffin" published in Family Tradition: A Bubba the Monster Hunter Prequel 2012

"9 Mystery Rose" published in Flesh and Bone: Rise of the Necromancers 2010

"Devil's Playground" published in Strange Tales of Horror 2011

"Hag Ride" published in Steamy Screams by Blood Bound Books 2011

"With the Turn of a Key" published in Dark Things V 2011

"Rhythm" published in Sirens Call eZine Women in Horror Month 2012

About the author

Eden Royce is a writer from Charleston, South Carolina whose great-aunt practiced root, a type of conjure magic. She now wishes she'd listened more closely.

She is also the horror submissions editor for Mocha Memoirs Press and a regular contributor to Graveyard Shift Sisters, a site dedicated to purging the Black female horror fan from the margins. In her dwindling free time, she reviews books for Hellnotes. She is also featured in the book, *60 Black Women in Horror Writing*.

Besides writing, her passions include roller-skating, listening to thunderstorms, and excellent sushi. Visit Eden's blog at darkgeisha.wordpress.com or her website at edenroyce.com.

You can also find her on Facebook as Eden Royce-The Dark Geisha and on Twitter @edenroyce.

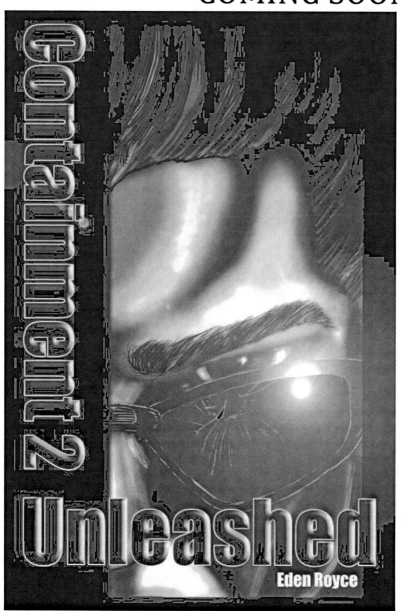